Robert Allen is sixty-five and this is his first book. He is an urbane and professional conversationalist who has spent the last forty years in exotic locations, working for an international oil company. Between 1964 and 1970 he lived in Tokyo and studied Japanese at tertiary level. He was also a member of trade missions to Japan in the mid-1980s. His next book for Imprint is set in Vietnam in the early 1960s and will be published in October 1990.

IMPRINT

# TOKYO
# NO HANA

## ROBERT ALLEN

PR
9619.3
.A468
T6
1990
c.2

## IMPRINT

ANGUS & ROBERTSON PUBLISHERS

First published in 1990 by Angus & Robertson Publishers
Unit 4, Eden Park, 31 Waterloo Road, North Ryde, NSW, Australia 2113;
and 16 Golden Square,
London WIR 4BN, United Kingdom

Copyright © Robert Allen, 1990

National Library of Australia
Cataloguing-in-Publication data:

Allen, Robert, 1924–
Tokyo no hana.
ISBN 0 207 16594 7.
I. Title.
A823.3

All rights reserved. No part of this publication may be reproduced,
stored in a retrieval system, or transmitted, in any form, or
by any means, electronic, mechanical, photocopying, recording or
otherwise, without the prior permission of the publishers.

This book is sold subject to the condition that it shall not,
by way of trade or otherwise, be lent, resold, hired out or
otherwise circulated without the publisher's prior consent
in a form of binding or cover other than that in which it is
published and without a similar condition including this condition
being imposed on the subsequent purchaser.

Typeset in 11pt Times Roman by Midland Typesetters, Victoria
Printed by Globe Press, Victoria

Cover illustration: *Her First Japanese Meal* by Brett Whiteley
Private collection

Creative writing programme assisted by the Australia Council,
the Australian government's arts advisory and support organisation.

For my Japanese friends past and present. With thanks to Viki Wright for her generous guidance.

# CONTENTS

*1* Prologue—Nakajima-sensei ... 1

*2* The Exodus from Manchuria ... 5

*3* The Second Wife ... 9

*4* The Donzoko ... 13

*5* The Intruder ... 18

*6* Tabi no Haji ... 23

*7* The Moon-View Noodles ... 27

*8* Season Off ... 32

*9* The Flowers of the Floating World ... 36

*10* Giri-Man ... 43

*11* Winter Snowstorm ... 50

*12* The Champs Elysées of Tokyo ... 59

*13* The Head Office Visitor ... 67

*14* Too Much Happy Time ... 74

*15* The Reaffirmation of Life ... 80

| | | |
|---|---|---|
| *16* | The Five-Year Marriage Contract | 83 |
| *17* | The Shōgatsu Pay-Off | 93 |
| *18* | Epilogue — High Blood | 101 |

# 1
# PROLOGUE
# NAKAJIMA-SENSEI

When Andrew Paton first saw Nakajima-sensei coming across the room towards him with the shuffling gait of a woman in kimono, bowing almost as she came, a small, plump old lady with brightly hennaed hair, quick eyes behind thick glasses and a wide, grinning mouth, she was so exactly like a caricature that his first impulse, unkind and misjudged, was to laugh.

He had not wanted to leave Kuala Lumpur and come to Japan but the transfer had been decided by his company, Radonics Ltd of Sydney, and all his arguments against it had been rejected. After five years in Kuala Lumpur he had become acclimatised to both the weather and the way of living and that was exactly the argument the Sydney office had used against him. He was only just over thirty years of age, they had reminded him, he was unmarried and mobile, he had the best part of his career before him and the Japanese operations of Radonics were expanding. This was his big opportunity. He should take it before he went completely native and merged into the Malaysian landscape. Unless of course, it was hinted darkly, he preferred to seek his fortune beyond the protective arms of the Radonics group.

It was true that he had become too well assimilated into Malaysian life; he had mastered the Malay language and spoke it fluently. He was unusually adaptable and felt at home wherever he found himself. But once ensconced in a new culture he had a great reluctance to pull up his roots and start again in another one. He thought of it in terms of writing-off a sound investment.

In Japan he found himself starting again from the bottom of the cultural ladder in a society which was almost as different from that of Malaysia as it was from that of his native Australia.

One of his first decisions had been to arrange for Japanese lessons, as the language barrier was immense, much greater than in Kuala Lumpur where, as the capital of a former British colony, English was ubiquitous.

His study of the Japanese language and culture soon became an all-consuming interest for him and he carried it into every aspect of his daily and nightly life. He eschewed the Press Club and the American Club, the haunts of the *gaijin* (foreigners) and avoided business lunches in such places. He had lunch every day in one or other of the small sushi restaurants in Tsukiji, near the fish market, or in Shimbashi, not far from the Ginza, and practised his Japanese on those around him. He eventually became quite a judge of sashimi and sushi, and acquired an extensive knowledge of the types of fish and seafood and the best places and seasons for them. Gaijin at that time almost universally avoided raw fish and it was extremely rare for him ever to encounter another non-Japanese in a sushi shop. It was to be many years before sushi, always the most expensive of all Japanese cuisine, was to sweep America by storm.

Andrew always carried in his coat pocket a small dictionary and a notebook in which he drew thumbnail sketches of places and people and wrote the words and expressions he had been unable to understand. With Nakajima he would later solve these puzzles and they would discuss his impressions. Nakajima was his willing accomplice, his guide in absentia.

She was a highly respectable person to the outside world and undoubtedly virtuous in her personal life as well. She was a Christian and a pillar of her church; she was cultivated; she played the koto with professional skill; she regularly sat through the entire season of Kabuki theatre and much of the Noh drama. Her ancestry was impeccable. But inside Nakajima was a joyful pagan with a hearty, bawdy lust for life which seemed never to have been gratified in practice and which she could enjoy vicariously in her conspiracy with Andrew to lay before him the treasures and mysteries of her language.

When Andrew first began to study Japanese he felt that he

## PROLOGUE—NAKAJIMA-SENSEI

was separated from the life around him by a barrier of incomprehension, as if an impenetrable wall surrounded him. Then, gradually, under Nakajima's instruction chinks of light appeared here and there and tiny doors seemed to open.

In a literal sense she did open the door for him. She would help him on with his coat, refusing to allow him to help her, and, if they were going out at the same time, open the door of his office and stand back to allow him to pass first. She would insist on carrying his briefcase and on walking behind him. At the elevator she would wait for him to enter, murmur her little phrase *'Dōzo o saki ni'* (please go ahead), and follow behind. When Andrew objected that this was not the way things were done in Australia, she replied firmly that this was not Australia. He finally gave up protesting.

She came to his office twice a week for lessons lasting from 12 noon until 2 p.m. After the first few months of oral lessons they began on the written language, and Andrew would walk around Tokyo translating everything he could read. It soon became clear from Nakajima's comments that she was encouraging him to have romantic involvements with Japanese girls who, she assured him, had a soft spot for gaijin, even if it were a *'hen na gaijin'* (a strange foreigner) like Andrew. This term was frequently disparaging but often indulgent, depending on the tone of voice, and reflected the ambivalent attitude of many Japanese towards foreigners who adapted themselves too well to Japanese ways and who professed a healthy interest in the country.

Nakajima took delight in Andrew's romances, real or imagined. Andrew also discovered that, in spite of her ingrained habits of deference to superiors and tolerance to inferiors, in reality Nakajima had little respect for anybody or anything, for any system or man-made institution. She was at heart a wayward hedonist, hemmed in from all sides by history, customs, traditions and her impecunious circumstances. Andrew recognised this and loved her for it and she loved him for his understanding of her. It was a platonic, intellectual friendship, seasoned with humour and sexual innuendo. She often said that she wished she were forty years younger; and there was no doubt that if she had been, their relationship would have developed differently.

Nakajima was married to a man whom she had followed to Manchuria when that country was ruled by the Japanese. After Japan's defeat in the war the couple had straggled back to their own country as penniless refugees and had settled in Osaka for some years before moving to Tokyo. Nakajima often spoke disparagingly of her husband—she resented his failure to provide for them both; she resented the total failure of his life. And yet she clung to him and deferred to his opinions and went home at night to tell him every detail of what she had found interesting during the day. He was a frail, thin person, bent with age, with a hawk nose and false teeth that joggled up and down when he spoke. He was very well educated and his failures had not been of his own doing but the result of turmoil and upheaval beyond his control. He had four or five different jobs during the years Andrew knew him, the last one being a sort of maître d'hôtel in a restaurant. Although old, he could not afford to stop work.

Nakajima's life had spread across the old and the new in Japan, from the strict, traditional upbringing and the tight network of obligation and counter-obligation which regulated almost every waking moment of the day, to the present time when many traditions, customs and thought patterns were being questioned, modified or abandoned. Nakajima explained many of these changes with regret and nostalgia. Others she applauded; and sometimes Andrew caught her out regretting and applauding the same thing.

She told him many stories and recounted many anecdotes to illustrate the meaning of words. She had an earthy sense of humour and would, with the air of a conspirator, tell Andrew the most scabrous carryings-on of her neighbours and friends.

Some of the stories that follow originate from Nakajima's gossip or from events in her own life; two of them were recounted to Andrew by a Japanese friend, Obata-sensei, and others reflect his own experience. All of them touch on some aspect of Japanese life.

# 2
# THE EXODUS FROM MANCHURIA

When Nakajima first married, her husband was working with the South Manchuria Railway Company in its hotel division. She went back to Manchuria with him after the wedding and they lived in the various towns where the hotels were situated—places from a lost era, with evocative names like Port Arthur, Mukden, Dairen and Hsinking.

Manchuria, then called Manchukuo, was governed by Japan under a puppet régime, glossed over with the pomp of high-sounding institutions and with a public relations policy that seems to have been more convincing and comforting to the Japanese themselves than to the world at large.

The spirit of the Rule was said to be Wang-tao, literally meaning the Ways of the King, implying benevolence, justice and humanity. Under the rule of Wang-tao there was to be no tyranny, no calamity of party strife, and all men were to become brothers, enjoying peace and happiness in perfect security.

While this desirable state of affairs prevailed, the country could be developed and its rich natural resources opened up. Nakajima had married late for a Japanese woman and had reached middle age in 1945 when the war ended and the Russians liberated Manchuria. There was a state of confusion at this time, she told Andrew, and many Japanese families living in Manchuria had already been evacuated to country towns, often leaving the husband at his job in the city. In Nakajima's case her husband had been evacuated with her, since his work in a tourist hotel had suddenly lost its importance.

It was during the hiatus between the imminence of invasion and the actual liberation of the country that the Nakajimas found themselves beginning to understand their fellow countrymen as real people, reduced to the elementary problem of living or dying, shorn of the politeness of social intercourse. They were in a small village, sharing a farmhouse with two other families. In the same village were some 250 Japanese, mainly women and children. There was limited food, the authority of the puppet régime was beginning to crumble into anarchy and the Chinese were becoming bolder and more intrusive.

Then invasion occurred and the Russians, having at least temporarily inherited the Japanese position, began to institute a puppet régime of their own. The new Chinese authorities sent an army squad into the town to round up all the able-bodied men for labour on the roads. No one knew if these men would ever return and so Nakajima, fearing for her husband's life, hid him in a hollow space between the ceiling of the farmhouse and the floor of the loft. He stayed there, coming out only briefly at night, for nearly three weeks. The house was searched several times but, as the Chinese did not know which Japanese wives had been evacuated alone and which had come accompanied, they did not suspect her unduly. Nevertheless, Nakajima lived those three weeks in dread lest one of the other Japanese women, seeking an advantage for herself, should betray her.

Then, as suddenly as the road-labour recruiting squad had arrived, it disappeared. The Japanese recruits did not come back and their wives and mothers heard no more of them until months later when some of them found each other again on ships leaving the country. Some of them never found each other again.

The order for total evacuation came. The Japanese in the village, now reduced to about 200 people, were to walk to Mukden. They set off early one summer morning. Nakajima said they were a sorry crew; some of the women whose men had disappeared were periodically hysterical, the children became tired, the grandmothers cried silently as they walked and one young woman gave birth to a baby by the side of the road. Only the presence of the Chinese coolies comforted them. Unconcerned as coolies are with politics and power, they carried the evacuees' bags and bundles in return for a small sum of money and in emergencies also carried the children and the elderly.

As they walked, they had to buy what little food was available. They slept where they could find shelter. They straggled forlornly into Mukden.

Mukden was a city situated on a vast plain looking out over the river Hung-ho. It consisted in those days of three parts: the Walled City, surrounded by a wall thirty-five feet high and broken by four towered gates; the International Settlement and the South Manchuria Railway Town. The evacuees were put in the International Settlement, along with several thousand others, to await shipment by rail to the coast.

There were delays and false starts, while they suffered hunger and sickness, the bitterness of defeat and the tragedy of loss.

They were told that they could take out of the country no more than a nominal amount of money and neither valuables nor jewellery. There was to be no compensation for loss of their possessions, their businesses, their careers. Every garment, bag and bundle was examined and valuables were confiscated. Both men and women had to strip and each body cavity was searched.

Those of the Japanese who had foreseen these events had converted whatever money they could raise into jewellery and precious stones. Nakajima and her husband had put everything they had into one large diamond. They had been late doing it, however, and the market was already disorganised. They knew they had paid many times more for it than they would have if they had bought it a year or so earlier. But there it was, their diamond, their one possession.

Nakajima was plump with rolls of fat around her waist and she conceived the idea of keeping the diamond in her navel, strapped in with a little adhesive plaster. This had proven a satisfactory storage place during the long trek to Mukden, but when she heard of the body searches she was seized with panic. They then kept the stone taped into the point of one of her husband's shoes.

Finally the day came when the Nakajimas and others were put on a train for the long trip to Hsinking and Dairen. They found themselves in cattle trucks. So many people were crammed into these trucks that there was only enough room for half of them to sit down. There were no toilets; they had no food except what they had carried with them or were able to buy from the ever-decreasing supplies along the route. Men, women and children were all together, fifty persons to a truck designed to carry ten head of cattle.

The train lumbered on by an indirect route, heading northeast from Mukden, before descending south again to the seaport of Dairen. With stops to let ordinary rail traffic through, with breakdowns in the engine, with delays to pick up more evacuees or to search again and again through belongings, the trip took five days and nights.

Nakajima and her husband had had no food at all for the last two days before they arrived at Dairen, where the ship was waiting. It was a Japanese ship and even though it was without comforts and the evacuees slept where they stood, on the decks, in the holds, anywhere, it was still the hand of salvation stretched out to them. And there was a little, a very little, rice to eat.

It was not a triumphant return to Japan. In some ways the pain only really began to be felt when they realised that, safe as they were, their world had been shattered. And in Japan itself there was the bitter resignation to defeat and the first steps to be taken on a long road into an unknown future.

In the midst of this despairing appraisal of what had happened and what might happen, the Nakajimas received a blow which was so much the last sting of the whip that Nakajima said she both laughed and cried. Their diamond was examined by a jeweller and pronounced valueless.

# 3
# THE SECOND WIFE

From their state of destitution after the war Nakajima and her husband gradually made their way back up the steep slope to an adequate, if modest, standard of living. This they achieved by sheer hard work, he toiling at two and sometimes three jobs at the same time and she teaching both Japanese to foreigners and the koto to her fellow countrywomen.

They were not ignored by their peers. As a result of their traditional upbringing, their good education and the families from which they had sprung, both Nakajima and her husband were accepted socially by certain persons of wealth and position, in spite of their relative poverty.

Nakajima had a good friend, the legal wife of an enterprising and wealthy grain-dealer named Takamatsu. Takamatsu-san was a jovial man and enterprising in more ways than one—notably he had accumulated over the years two extra wives, not legally married wives but socially acceptable nonetheless. They were his *nigō-san* and his *sangō-san* (Wife Number Two and Wife Number Three). Each of these additions to his treasure had been made at moments of boredom or impatience or just frustration with the existing wife. Each was about fifteen years younger than her predecessor and each in turn had rekindled his ardour; but whereas his successive wives were younger, he himself was not and he had become an old man by the time the story began.

The first wife had had two children, the second wife four and the third two. The original family home, occupied by Madam Takamatsu, was in Azabu. The second wife had a house in Akasaka not far from the Okura Hotel and the third wife an apartment in Roppongi. These places are quite close to each other, so Takamatsu was able to minimise his travelling time and conserve his energies for where they were most needed.

For many years Madam Takamatsu had eaten her heart out over this arrangement and it seems that she never grew to accept it. She was jealous of the two others and would tell Nakajima joyfully of the mishaps that befell them. She particularly resented the second wife who, she said, was flighty and had had affairs with other men. These infidelities enraged Madam Takamatsu, who believed that such disloyalty to her husband was adding insult to injury. Nor was the situation made any better by the fact that she herself had grown too old and unattractive to emulate her rival. For her, as the real wife, to have had love affairs would have been a far more serious infringement of the social code than for the second and third de factos.

So Madam Takamatsu had lived out her life and learned to play the koto, had taken examinations in flower arranging and had gone away for weekend trips to the mountains with her women friends. She had told Nakajima how the children from the three families were doing at school and how those of the second wife were badly behaved, which was only to be expected, of course. Such information was supplied to Madam Takamatsu by the servants of the various houses, as she had never personally set eyes on her rivals.

Then one day Madam Takamatsu died. Her two children were grown up and presented no problem, but the matter of property and inheritance came up because old Takamatsu-san himself suddenly had a vision of his own mortality. He made suitable financial arrangements for the first wife's two children and he married the second wife.

Nakajima had never met the second wife but she lost no time in calling on her, paying her respects and leaving a present. The second wife who, in spite of her previously flighty ways, was at heart a traditionalist, immediately took to Nakajima and they became firm friends. The second wife also had some confidences she wished to share. It appeared that, while regarding old Madam Takamatsu as a tedious bore from whom she had taken her husband as an act of charity, she had never been able to reconcile herself to the presence of the third wife. This woman, Nakajima

## THE SECOND WIFE

learned, was a hussy—a modern girl who had a university degree, loved Western music and had obviously seduced old man Takamatsu with a heady mixture of culture (to enchant his mind) and the performance of uninhibited sexual gymnastics on the futon (to delight his waning passions).

That these passions had indeed been revived was evidenced by the birth of two children in rapid succession after which no more appeared, and the second wife was often tortured by the thought that this was probably due more to contraception than to any diminution of old man Takamatsu's enthusiasm.

And so the second wife bore her cross, which did not become lighter when she was finally legally married, although she was happy to feel at last that firm provision had been made for her children.

Then, unexpectedly, after a long and productive life, old man Takamatsu's vision of mortality materialised. He died one night after a geisha party in Tsukiji, near the fish market of Tokyo.

After this mournful event the third wife seems to have gone off the rails and Nakajima would bring stories of the severe disapproval with which the second wife regarded the love affairs of this lonely young woman. Such behaviour was an insult to the memory of old man Takamatsu, she said, and was not to be tolerated. Of course, it must be remembered that by this time the second wife had lost her appeal to other men and, while this may not have mattered while she still had a husband, it did matter now that she did not.

It was Nakajima who suggested the solution to the problem and Nakajima's husband—frail, dignified and indefatigable—who carried it out. This solution was to find a suitable husband for the third wife. The second wife thought this a splendid idea but the third wife, who was modern and free, did not take kindly to it. However, Nakajima, who had never met the third wife before, called on her with a present, and after a short exchange of courtesies broached the subject of the marriage. There was an appropriate man in mind, a nephew of old man Takamatsu, whose own wife had died very young. Nakajima said that her husband had had much experience as a go-between in arranging marriages and that he would be willing to introduce the parties and attend to all the details. The case in favour of the marriage was financial. It would assure the future of the third wife's two children and it would also keep the property in the Takamatsu family. And so it happened that when the third wife was introduced to old man Takamatsu's nephew, she immediately liked him. The marriage took place and Nakajima heard that it was very happy.

One day soon after the wedding Nakajima came to show Andrew a beautiful little jade vase that she had received from the second wife as a token of her gratitude. Now, it seemed, with all the family's problems solved and honour saved, the second wife reigned supreme. She was perhaps a little lonely at times but she had her four children and on special occasions would hold family parties for all old man Takamatsu's progeny, including the grown-up ones who would bring their children and those of the third wife who was now also a Madam Takamatsu in her own right and seemed to have decided against contraception after all.

Nakajima said this always made a pretty big family party.

# 4
# THE DONZOKO

Andrew very rarely met Nakajima socially, but on one occasion he was unable to have his usual lesson at the office and he invited her to have dinner with him in Shinjuku instead.

This was very much a student quarter at that time with none of the huge Western-style hotels which have recently raised its skyline. It was a rabbit-warren of night-life, with countless bars, restaurants, cabarets, Turkish bath houses, strip joints, cinemas and theatres.

Andrew occasionally took foreign friends to Shinjuku. Most of them, even long-term Tokyo residents, had never ventured there alone. The half-hour taxi ride from central Tokyo before the oil shocks of the 1970s cost between 300 and 400 yen. The reason therefore for foreigners not attempting to go to Shinjuku was not the cost of the fare but the fact that it was almost essential to speak Japanese in order to enjoy the place.

On this occasion Andrew took Nakajima on a culinary hashigo. Hashigo, the word for ladder, is also the term used for pub crawl, the inference being that, as one drinks in one pub after another, one climbs higher and higher. Andrew's version of the hashigo comprised a dinner in which each course was taken at a different small restaurant opening onto the street.

He remembered the first few times he had stood on the edge of the bustling crowd, nervously touching the sliding door of a tiny restaurant and summoning up his courage to open it and go in. Surprised Japanese faces had turned in his direction as he entered, the proprietor had courteously called out the customary phrase of welcome, as if by reflex action, and then there had been an uneasy silence. Conversations had stopped. Andrew had felt a furious impulse to turn on his tail and run. It was as if he had entered a club of which he were not a member—indeed, some of the tiny bars were clubs at which non-members, particularly foreigners, were unwelcome. But he had always persevered, smiling and uttering a polite Japanese phrase, taking his place on a stool at the counter behind which the owner was preparing food and warming the sake. Curiosity would soon get the better of his neighbours at the counter and they would ask a tentative question. Then, little by little, almost imperceptibly, relations would warm up. Often at the end of the meal he and his fellow customers would be filling up each other's sake cups and exchanging name cards. It was the best possible way to learn the language.

The hashigo with Nakajima began at a sushi shop where they had sashimi and hot sake, continued on to a yakitori place where they ate a few sticks of charcoal-grilled chicken and drank more sake, then on further to an unagiya for grilled eel, again with sake, and finally to a coffee shop where Nakajima devoured a large piece of cake covered in cream and Andrew had a cold beer. Nakajima said that she normally did not drink much sake and that she felt a little the worse for it tonight.

Andrew then suggested going to the Donzoko to sing and observe the crowd. The narrow streets in the vicinity of the Donzoko were so much alike in their vivid decoration of neon lights, hanging lanterns and lighted bar signs that it took Andrew some time to locate it. From the outside it looked like an old castle, hemmed in on both sides by buildings ablaze with neon from street to roof. Inside there was a winding stone staircase leading from the ground floor to the third floor past scenes of revelry. On the third floor there was a piano and a microphone and crowds of customers sitting, drinking, laughing, talking loudly and occasionally joining in with whoever was singing into the microphone. Waiters and waitresses jostled with each other and with the customers coming and going on the stairs. The atmosphere was one of excitement and gaiety.

All the tables were full but some students made room for them and they sat down. Each table sat many people, the number depending on how tightly they bunched together on the benches.

## THE DONZOKO

The effect was to eliminate privacy. Andrew was the only gaijin at the Donzoko that night and the students at their table wanted to talk to him to practise their English and to hear him speak Japanese. There were both male and female students at the table, as well as a couple in their forties, visibly in love, who were more reticent than the students and were being teased by them in a good-natured way. Everyone drank freely. Andrew ordered a stein of beer and Nakajima had a cup of coffee.

The students complimented Andrew on the wisdom of bringing his grandmother along to protect him from temptation, to which Nakajima replied with a stinging attack on the lack of respect of the present generation, coupled with some witty remarks which brought hoots of laughter. One of the girl students insisted on sitting beside her and another offered her a crème de menthe liqueur in a tiny glass which, in spite of her caution, Nakajima drank and enjoyed.

The girl student sitting beside her soon discovered that Nakajima could sing traditional Japanese songs and she was prevailed upon to stand in front of the microphone and sing. The audience applauded enthusiastically. A student from another table then sang a Russian revolutionary song and everyone on the third floor joined in, reading the words from booklets which were on the tables. This was followed by a series of drinking songs and ultimately Andrew sang 'Waltzing Matilda'.

By this time Nakajima had drunk several glasses of crème de menthe and, when they decided to leave at midnight, Andrew and the girl student had to help her down the stairs. Outside in the street the crowd had thinned out and people were going home. Most of them, like Andrew and Nakajima, had started their evening at 6 p.m. Taxis were taking people out of the entertainment district and returning for more. Other people were walking to the underground stations to catch the last train home. Shinjuku was winding down the party for yet another night. There were some places in Tokyo that stayed open till 2 or 3 a.m. but most of them were in the Roppongi district where Andrew lived.

Outside in the cool midnight air Nakajima seemed even less steady on her feet than she had been in the Donzoko. The girl student, whose name was Eiko, said goodnight to her friends and proposed to go with Andrew and Nakajima and put Nakajima to bed. As she pointed out, Andrew could not undress Nakajima himself and Nakajima's husband would be more understanding of the situation if another woman accompanied her. If Nakajima's husband were asleep, Eiko would undress her and see her comfortably into her futon.

They had to wait some time for a taxi but were eventually driven to Nakajima's apartment in Shibuya. Andrew waited downstairs in the taxi while Eiko took Nakajima inside. Ten minutes or so later she reappeared, smiling. Nakajima's husband had been, and still was, sound asleep, snoring loudly. Eiko said that it was rather funny really, because he snored and whistled alternately.

She had undressed Nakajima down to the second last layer of the voluminous garments under her kimono and had piloted her to the futon beside her husband. No sooner had she been rolled into place than she too began to snore and her snores and whistles seemed to be in time with those of her husband.

Eiko sat in the back of the taxi with Andrew telling him all this, while the taxi-driver waited and listened patiently. Eiko was a very pretty girl in her early twenties. She had kind eyes. Andrew told her this and she put her hand on his knee, shaking her head in dissent. Then she leaned over towards him slightly and, as if mesmerised by her eyes, he bent forward and kissed her on the lips. She responded.

After a while the taxi-driver, hearing no more conversation, turned around to see what was happening. Andrew and Eiko were kissing, oblivious of his presence. He turned back to the steering wheel, coughed softly and asked, 'Where to now?'

It was Eiko who answered, giving him the name of a small love-hotel in Harajuku, and the driver set off without a word.

The hotel, a Japanese-style inn, was set in a small garden of rocks and pine trees, almost like a bonsai arrangement. They were welcomed cheerfully by a woman in a kimono who asked only how long they would require the room.

'*San jikan gurai,*' Eiko replied. (About three hours.)

They were led along winding passages to a room with a tiny bathroom beside it in which a hot bath had already been run. Japanese tea was brought and set down on the low table between them as they sat cross-legged on the tatami matting. A double futon bed had been made up in an alcove of the room, the clean sheets folded back invitingly. As soon as the maid had left them alone with the tea, they undressed and squeezed into the bath tub together. Eiko laughed at the hair on Andrew's chest, running her fingers through it and telling him he looked like a bear.

Andrew asked her why she had stipulated three hours.

'Oh,' she said, 'it's always pleasant not to have to rush things and, besides, I want to talk to you afterwards. Perhaps you will be my good friend, my gaijin bear!'

'We'll probably fall asleep.'

'In that case three hours is good. They won't have any customers at four o'clock in the morning and they'll let us sleep until we wake. Do you have enough money for breakfast?'

'I think so.'

'Andrew-chan, how lucky I am! My gaijin bear can pay for my breakfast. Wasn't it sad that Nakajima-sensei had to be taken home? She really shouldn't have drunk so much but this now, here in the bath with you, I mean, is *fukōchū no saiwai* [cloud with silver lining]. If she had refused the crème de menthe, what could I have done to enchant you?'

'But it wasn't you who bought her the crème de menthe, Eiko.'

'Yes it was, Andrew-chan, I gave my friend the money to pay for them, otherwise I could buy *you* breakfast.'

'You planned the whole thing then?'

'Yes, as soon as I saw you.'

'I thought Japanese women were modest and unassuming.'

'You are just learning about us. Besides, I am nearly finished at university. What good is it to have a scientific education and not to use your brains?'

# 5
# THE INTRUDER

Nakajima used to say that there were three classes of dishonest businessmen in Japan: real estate agents, land developers and the owners of pet shops. In Australia, Andrew would object, pet shop owners were considered uncontroversial. Not so in her country, said Nakajima. Then darkly, 'they', the pet shop owners, were often backed up by the gangster element or by Koreans. These two were of equal awfulness in Nakajima's mind.

It was therefore all the more surprising when one day Nakajima told Andrew she had bought a dog from a well-known pet shop in the Ginza. She had bought it on impulse, without consulting her husband, without knowing anything about how to care for it and without having the money to pay for it.

It was apparently a pure bred something or other and had cost 80 000 yen, payable 10 000 yen as deposit and 7000 yen per month for ten months. Nakajima had had just enough for the deposit and had taken the dog home with a little pamphlet on the care of animals, rather, Andrew imagined, like the brochure one gets from a nursery on how to plant a tree.

At that time it was fashionable to be seen walking a dog in Tokyo. Dogs were bought as ornaments. Rare dogs, expensive dogs, tiny dogs, huge dogs, were being imported from overseas, particularly from England. But the difference between the attitude of the English (whose obsession with dogs was nonetheless not allowed to stifle the desire to make a profit from their export) and that of the Japanese was most marked. Put simply, the Japanese did not regard the acquisition of a pet animal as a life-long commitment. This distinction they reserved for their wives. Andrew sometimes felt that the English attitude was the reverse.

It would be wildly overstating the case to say that Japan and the United Kingdom came close to breaking off diplomatic relations over the treatment of dogs but there was a lot of emotive publicity in the press on both sides. Andrew's friend, Professor Jenkins, an English resident in Tokyo, formed a protection of dogs association and bombarded the Japan *Times*, the *Yomiuri* and the *Mainichi*, all English-language newspapers, with long, carefully worded and furious letters. He protested at the treatment of pure-bred English dogs which had been imported to Japan and sold to customers who, having tired of the novelty, discarded them or gave them away, like old clothes, to someone else who in turn also discarded them. Visits were made to the dog pounds by groups of biased persons on both sides of the argument and these visits produced opposite results of equal force. From the dog fanciers' side came photos of Belsen-camp dimensions which were published in newspapers back in England and inspired wrathful questions in the House of Commons. From the Japanese side came photos of dogs in the pounds playing happily and eating huge plates of food (which the English said was rice). The Japanese also pointed out that the mechanism for destruction of unclaimed dogs had now benefited from an injection of modern technology and was swift and painless (errors and omissions excepted).

In the end the Japanese threatened to prohibit further importation of dogs from England. This delighted Professor Jenkins and his friends but not the exporters in the United Kingdom. Such is the magnetism of the export dollar that in the face of economic reality the dispute was allowed, or rather encouraged, to cool off.

Nakajima acquired her dog in the middle of the furore. Her husband was shocked. They had never had a dog before. They lived in a tiny two-room apartment with tatami floors everywhere except the kitchen. They had no bathroom but used the neighbourhood public bath. There was no balcony. Where, he wanted to know, were they to put the dog?

According to the famous pet shop from which it had been bought, the dog was fully house-trained. So the old couple found a large cardboard carton, lined it with towels and put the dog in it to sleep. They then unfolded their futon from the cupboard where it was stored during the day, spread it out on the tatami and went to bed.

For a while on the first night all seemed to be well. Then in the dark they could hear the dog moving about and scratching. Tatami matting is made from straw. The mats are six feet long and three feet wide and about two inches thick. The bulk of the thickness is rough straw, tightly compressed, but the top covering is finely woven and smooth to the touch. It is not improved by being scratched by a dog. The Nakajimas switched on the lights and inspected the damage, which was fortunately not extensive; they tied the dog up with an old belt and put him back in the carton. Then they went to sleep.

During the night, old man Nakajima had a dream. In it he was lolling on a tropical island in the sun. Then the clouds rolled over and it began to rain softly, warmly, on his bald head. When he woke, he found it had not been a dream after all. Not only had the dog, after chewing through the belt, made his mark on old man Nakajima's head, but he had also claimed as his own almost every object in the two rooms. It was disaster.

The next night they locked him in the kitchen. From the moment the door closed behind them until the next morning, the dog whined and howled. It was a long, pleading, heart-breaking howl, rising to a high pitch and descending pathetically to a whimper. Every other occupant of the apartment building lodged a complaint and the landlord threatened the Nakajimas with eviction. Beside this menace a state of utter chaos in the kitchen was of relatively minor importance.

On the third night they decided that preventive measures were necessary. And so at midnight old man Nakajima took the dog for a walk in the streets. They put him to bed in the kitchen, but with the door open, and set the alarm for 2 a.m., when Nakajima herself took him for a walk. At 4 a.m. and at 6 a.m. they followed the same procedure, turn and turn about.

When they awoke at 7.30 a.m., exhausted after the broken night's sleep, they found the kitchen floor aflood and patches of wet in four or five other parts of the apartment. In addition, as Nakajima had unwisely fed the dog on fish and rice the previous evening, it had been sick in front of the television set.

This was the end. She decided to take the dog back to that bright, shining, opulent-looking pet shop in the Ginza. She arrived, having carefully prepared her little speech in the most polite way, with the dog on a new lead. She was, she said, extremely sorry to have put them to so much trouble but, as the health of her husband had suddenly deteriorated and one or two other unforeseen complications had arisen, she was unable to keep the dog. She realised that it was only fair for her to forfeit the 10 000 yen she had paid and she hoped they would take back the dog and cancel the time payment contract.

But whereas in selling Nakajima the dog the shop assistants had been the acme of politeness and consideration, now the situation was reversed. She was informed very coldly that animals could not be returned; they had become second hand. How could they know what she had fed the dog? If they took it back, it might die tomorrow. Furthermore, a contract was a contract and they would sue her for the remaining 70 000 yen.

On this day a most wretched Nakajima came to Andrew's office and instead of a lesson she poured out her worries. Together they worked out a little stratagem. There was a police box down the street from the pet shop and the plan was for Nakajima to go there with the dog, act like a very confused and lost old lady (which she resembled at that moment anyway) and with her female wiles, grandmotherly as they were, persuade one of the policemen to see her to the pet shop and leave her at the glass door where she would be visible to all inside. The Tokyo policemen are generally very pleasant people and ready to help.

The plan worked. When she entered the shop there was quite a marked improvement on her reception earlier in the day. She explained that she had been to the police to seek their advice on what she felt was a case of exploitation of an old and ignorant woman by slick young businessmen. The police, she said, had advised her to try once more to negotiate by herself, and if that failed they would be prepared to make an investigation and possibly provide her with free legal services.

For the form of it, for face-saving purposes, the shop assistant and the shop manager repeated what they had said earlier, but they then said that, on observing the dog more closely, it was clear he was in good health and had not been mistreated. One had to be so careful these days, they said, when the standard of honesty of the community did not measure up to Japanese traditions. Now that they knew her better and realised what a fine, upright woman she was, they felt a compromise could be effected.

It was. The shop took back the dog on condition that Nakajima paid a further 8000 yen in four monthly instalments. If the dog were resold at its original price before the expiration of the four months, the payments would cease. This last part would be impossible for Nakajima to prove and presumably was included for window-dressing.

When all was settled and the dog handed over, Nakajima came back to Andrew to report on her success. It was then that Andrew felt a severe lecture on extravagance was called for, and he delivered it. Now, he pointed out, she had to pay 2000 yen a month for four months for absolutely nothing.

But female logic does not work that way. As to the 2000 yen, Nakajima said, that was 5000 yen less than she would have had to pay under the original contract and for only four months instead of ten. So she was making a profit. And then again, she said with enormous conviction, until you have actually had a dog in your apartment you cannot possibly realise that it's worth 2000 yen a month *not* to have one!

# 6
# TABI NO HAJI

There is a saying in Japanese that *'Tabi no haji wa kakisute'*. This means that when travelling you may do things you would be ashamed to do at home. Perhaps they are little things, like drinking too much and forgetting your manners, or perhaps there may be one thing, one event which when you return home remains locked in your heart, never to be revealed. In any case, as the event was final and complete in itself, finished and to all intents and purposes forgotten, it can be stored away in that repository of experiences which we call the past. Life continues, other sunrises, other days, other voyages.

With or without peccadilloes, travel in Japan usually starts out joyfully. In the second-class carriages of the crowded holiday trains there is always a noisy throng of men, women and children eating, talking, laughing, playing games and drinking. In hot weather the men often strip down to their long underwear for coolness and comfort. Girls wheel trolleys up and down the central aisle of the train, selling *mikan* (mandarins), *o-bentō* (boxes of food, usually with rice), cold beer, sake, whisky and sweets. The whole atmosphere is one of relaxation. Peanut shells, beer cans, mandarin peel and used plastic teacups are placed or thrown on the floor (depending on temperament and degree of insouciance) and the mess the train sweepers remove is mountainous. These things seem to set the mood of tabi no haji. One does not throw peanut shells on the floor at home; the release from the ordinary has begun.

For reasons of hierarchy and face, behaviour in the first-class compartments is more restrained but the same amenities are enjoyed.

Early one summer Andrew was travelling with a group of Japanese in the Limited Express from Tokyo to Sendai in Tohoku.

His Japanese friends were members of a *kai*, or association, and their objective was a sightseeing trip to Matsushima. The Limited Express to Sendai took five and a half hours, passing through flat ricefields and, later, forests and hills which all winter long had been covered in snow and were now green and vibrant.

From Sendai the party drove by car to Shiogama to catch one of the ferryboats across the Matsushima bay to the town of the same name. This bay is one of the three classic scenic spots of Japan. It is dotted with hundreds of tiny islands, their bases eroded by the action of the sea into strange shapes like archways and inverted pinnacles. Each of these islands is covered in pine trees and these have also grown into exotic, graceful shapes. The name Matsushima comes from the words for pine (*matsu*) and island (*shima*).

From the high ground on the Shiogama side of the bay there are places for viewing this scene. If the water is very still and the sky gently overcast, as it often is, the effect is ethereal. Then, when you bend down with your head between your legs and look at it upside down, the reflections of the islands in the water are so clear that the view is almost the same as it is right side up.

When the ferryboat arrived it meandered through these islands in a silence broken only by the throb of the engines, the prattle of the passengers and the clicking of cameras until it came to its destination, Matsushima town. Just in front of the town is an island with a temple, connected to the mainland by an arched red bridge; and nearby are the landing quays for the ferries.

The party disembarked, took taxis to their *ryokan* (Japanese-style inn) and began the evening ritual of soaking together in the *ōfuro*, the large communal hot bath, followed by the supreme luxury of sitting in cotton kimonos on the tatami floor, drinking beer and sake. Later the maids brought in trays of food, all the local specialities of the region.

It had been a long day and they were tired. Andrew went to his room and called for a massage before sleep.

The women who massage the guests of a country inn are

often blind. They are led to the room, where the guest is lying on his futon, and then left for an hour to knead his muscles. If the guest falls asleep in the process, the massage woman, or *ama-san*, collects her money at the front desk.

The ama-san who came to Andrew's room was indeed blind. Her eyes were clouded over. She had a sad face, almost beautiful in a way, and the effect of those clouded eyes in that face was one of inexpressible tragedy.

Andrew lay down on his side and her fingers began their rhythmic pattern of squeezing and releasing, probing, rubbing and squeezing again. The tiredness of the day's travel began to evaporate. He dropped off to sleep momentarily and woke to find that the girl was stroking his face, feeling with her hands for the shape of his features. He lay quite still.

Then, unexpectedly, she bent down, placed her head softly against his, her arms around his neck and held him. He felt warm tears falling on his cheek. The blind eyes were crying.

Andrew had never heard of a blind ama-san acting in this way and so he lay there, pretending to be asleep.

Outside the room the inn was very quiet. There was a soft flapping of a shutter somewhere and the wind was blowing in from the bay. He had no idea what time it was. He was an isolated human being in a quiet room, and another human being was crying in loneliness.

Almost in a trance, without desire but with the strength of one exerting all his might to save another, he took her in his arms. Her response was so fiercely passionate that for an instant the spell was broken. Then he realised that her blindness must be like a prison wall holding her sexual passions in check. He tried to be gentle with her but she would not let him. She clung to him and arched and strained against him until her whole body shook violently and he put his hand gently over her mouth to muffle her cries. Their lovemaking had been for her, not for him. His role had been that of the instrument for her pleasure and he was surprised he had been able to play this role without being caught up in her excitement.

When she was calm again, she sat up and began to massage his neck. Soon afterwards the sliding door opened and someone came to lead her away. Just as she left, she turned in Andrew's direction and smiled. For an uncanny moment he felt that she could see.

The next morning Andrew slid back the shutters and looked out on Matsushima bay. There was the red bridge to his left, stretching across to the island with the temple, the still, grey-blue sea and the haze of the sky. The wind had dropped.

The group returned to Tokyo later that afternoon. In the train Andrew was very quiet. He hardly noticed the noise and bustle around him and his thoughts were confused, a strange mixture of visions of beauty and of an inexplicable reaching out and touching another human being's heart. And yet had he really been the ministering angel he imagined himself to have been? Had he really reached out beyond himself to another? Can a dream in a quiet room at night be only an intangible wisp of memory the following morning?

The train sped on. The trip was over, with its release from routine, its change from the normal day-to-day life.

And locked in his heart, never to be revealed, was his *tabi no haji*.

# 7
# THE MOON-VIEW NOODLES

Noodles are an institution in Japan as firmly rooted as the national flag. There is wide variety in their method of preparation and, accordingly, an eating-house that makes noodles often makes nothing else. Such a shop is called a *sobaya*, because noodles come either in the form of *soba* (buckwheat noodles) or *sōmen* and *udon* (made from flour). At night you may buy soba from a *yatai*, or street stall, but for the full range of choice you must go to a sobaya.

Nakajima had another language student called von Brink who fell under the spell of the noodle and, with Teutonic thoroughness, devoted much time and energy to exploring the subject. He learned to order *kake soba* (the simplest form), *kitzune soba* (named after the fox), *tempura soba* (with deep-fried prawns on top), *zaru soba* (cold green noodles to be dipped in a sauce) and many others. But the particular dish that captured his imagination was *tsukimi soba*, a bowl of soba with a fried egg on top. The characters for this are those of the moon (*tsuki*) and the verb to see *(mi)*.

Von Brink discussed this interesting association of ideas with Nakajima and decided that a suitable translation would be 'moon-view noodles'.

In acquiring expertise as an eater of soba there was one difficult feat that von Brink took many months to master. This was the art of the slurp. In Japan it is not good manners to eat soba silently. With each mouthful a noisy intake of air must be made, producing a sound somewhere between a gargle and a hiss. When a dozen people are sitting around the bar counter of a soba shop, all with a single-minded determination to slurp up noodles with chopsticks, the musical effect can be either mesmerising or maddening.

Von Brink's first efforts at imitating this traditional sound were quite traumatic. Either the noise he made was so loud that all eyes were turned upon him, or he lost impetus while sucking up the strands of noodle, with the result that they fell back with a splash into his bowl. He ruined several neckties in this way.

Nevertheless, he persevered. He read translations of some famous Japanese stories about soba and would quote a geisha poem that reads:

> *shin shu shin nano no*
> *shin soba yori mo*
> *watashiya anata no*
> *soba ga yoi.*

With Nakajima's help he translated this as 'More than the fresh soba of Karuizawa [a mountain resort] for me your soba is best', a play on words meaning 'being close to you is best'.

It was when von Brink began to see the romance of soba that misfortune befell him. He had taken to eating frequently in a little sobaya in Kanda, just north of central Tokyo. It was mid-winter, very cold, and his wife was away in Germany with the von Brink children. He would sit at the counter in a corner of this minuscule shop, drinking hot sake long after he had finished eating, dreading the cold outside, the bleak taxi ride home and the empty apartment that awaited him.

The wife of the *sobaya-san* (the owner of the shop) was a plump little woman in her forties, cheerful and outgoing. She would tease him about his knowledge of soba, occasionally share some of his sake, and generally keep up an unending patter of small talk with him and her other customers.

She would look at von Brink's bald head, with its egg-shaped crown, and think how much it reminded her of tsukimi soba. She would look at his pale blue eyes, rather opaque behind metal-framed spectacles, his colourless eyebrows, his pallid skin, and she would wonder how any woman could ever have been attracted to him. And yet she felt sorry for him and in a strange way drawn to him. And so it happened that one night when it was particularly cold and her husband had gone to Ōsaka for a two-

## THE MOON-VIEW NOODLES

month stay, she took pity on him and, when the shop closed, led him upstairs.

This little romance was still continuing and von Brink was, as it were, sleeping on a bed of moon-view noodles in the tender arms of the wife of the sobaya-san, when Frau von Brink made her return to Japan. She did not come back because she passionately desired to be at her husband's side but because any further delay in Germany would make her family suspect that something was wrong with her marriage.

She arrived without the children, who had been installed in a good school, but with her two beloved dogs. According to Nakajima these dogs were enormous and were the only privileged residents of the household. They were the delight of Frau von Brink's life. She never stopped talking about them, brushing them, feeding them, walking them and chattering to them. On the other hand she scarcely addressed a word to von Brink.

In the past, when a similar situation had prevailed, von Brink had retired behind his papers, his pale eyes concentrated, his empty face expressionless. But now, for the first time, he began to react. Nakajima reported a most strained atmosphere in the von Brink ménage and with her unquenchable curiosity about anything that was not her business she took every opportunity of asking seemingly innocent but highly leading questions of both von Brink and his wife separately. She soon pieced the story together.

There were, it seems, constant fights and arguments about the dogs. It was not that the dogs were standing between husband and wife, since neither wanted to be together anyway, but rather that the dogs provided them with a focal point for their dissension, a battleground on which to vent their anger.

Now in Tokyo there is an organisation feared by all dog owners. This is the Dog Pound. In an active and energetic effort to keep stray dogs off the streets, dog-catching vans cruise around side streets picking up any dog without a collar, identification tags and a licence number. These dogs are then taken to the pound and, if not claimed within a week or so, destroyed. Some say the new destruction process is less efficient than it is claimed to be and, whether this is so or not, the thought that it may be acts as a spur to make dog owners pay their licence fees and keep their animals at home.

Seeing the dog-catcher van one day gave von Brink the idea for his revenge. It was extremely rare for Frau von Brink to separate from the two dogs, but the opportunity finally came and von Brink removed their collars (with the collection of little metal tags so vital to the dogs' security), and set them loose in the streets. That night he spent with the wife of the sobaya-san, who was still in Osaka, and he did not return to his apartment until the following day.

By that time Frau von Brink had been through a great deal of anger, anguish, misery and despair. She had in fact thought of the dog pound but telephone calls made by the servants on her behalf had only resulted in that peculiar form of non-answer so perfected by Japanese officialdom. Frau von Brink had been invited to come and look for herself—which she certainly intended to do, but a drive to the edge of the vast city of Tokyo was likely to be a time-consuming ordeal and there was no certainty that the dogs had been impounded in such a short time.

Von Brink then proposed his terms: simply that, if she would take her dogs and herself back to Germany and stay there, he would help her find them, but if she did not, he would do the same thing again and again until she did. With what can only mildly be described as acrimony, the terms were accepted.

And so it happened that Frau von Brink was forced to face the truth of her life and von Brink was soon to face the truth of his; because a week or so after his wife's departure, when von Brink had comfortably taken up his place at the corner of the counter in the soba shop and was rediscovering the joys of drinking sake and looking with anticipation at the plump form of the sobaya-san's wife, the sobaya-san himself came back triumphant from Osaka where he had arranged with his brother-in-law to open a branch shop.

The atmosphere in the shop is still gay and animated, von Brink often sits there, wondering about his empty apartment; and the sobaya-san's wife looks at von Brink's bald head (which does remind her of moon-view noodles) and she smiles. When she thinks at all of her passing fancy, it is with the inner amusement of one who has enjoyed an adventure and come through unscathed.

# 8
# SEASON OFF

From time to time Nakajima used to go away for a few days' holiday with women friends from her church or with other language teachers. The practice of travelling in groups is very common in Japan where society tends to be more collective and less individual than in the West. Perhaps twice a year the members of a government department, a business firm or an industrial association, for example, make trips to hot springs in the mountains, or go to the seaside, or to another one of the Japanese islands. And students who have graduated together from school or university will have an annual get-together for practically the rest of their lives. To cultivate and maintain one's personal relationships is regarded as of the highest importance.

Nakajima was never rich but she was extravagant from time to time and this meant that she was usually short of money. She would therefore always choose the place and the hotel with great care and then do a deal with the innkeeper to get a discount for the group.

So it happened that in January one year she and five other Japanese language teachers went to Lake Kawaguchi, or Kawaguchiko, for two days.

Kawaguchiko is one of the five lakes near Mount Fuji and is a popular summer resort. In winter its open-air icerink teems with weekend skaters and, when the lake freezes over and the hills are white with snow, it again becomes a magnet for tourists. However, in the month of January, before the heavy snowfalls, there is an off-season. This term seems to have entered the Japanese language as 'season off'.

There is something rather macabre about Kawaguchiko during the season off. The lake itself is still and grey under the grey sky. Around the shoreline, where black rocks finger out like serrated edges, the water is covered with thin ice, almost but not quite thick enough to walk on. In the morning on a fine day there is a pale sun which slants over the mountains, casting wide, black shadows on the surface of part of the lake and illuminating the other part, so that it reflects the clouds above. The sun creeps up the hillside, catching here and there patches of snow among the pine trees or frozen puddles on the road. It is cold and in mid-week the town is practically empty.

Nakajima and her friends stayed at an old hotel beside the lake. It was not a Japanese inn, although it compromised by having some Japanese-style rooms with tatami matting. It was not really a Western-style hotel either, at least not in the modern way. It was a magnificent old building, inspired probably by a mountain chalet in Austria or Switzerland and gently transformed into something unique with a Japanese tiled roof and gables and a Japanese garden with a torii gate near the entrance.

Among the party was an old lady named Masuta-san. Masuta-san differed from the rest of the group in two ways: first, she was quite rich, and second, she was very mean. Her meanness took the form of spending on herself and yet studiously avoiding spending on anyone else. At lunch, making a face-saving remark about her health, she would order an expensive meal for herself, while the others ate simple dishes of noodles or rice. In the hotel she had a room to herself, while the others shared three or more to the room. When it came to present-giving occasions, her gifts were calculated down to the minimum acceptable limit. All of this would have been bearable, however irritating, if it had not been for her unfortunate habit of conveniently never having change to pay her share of communal expenses, like taxi fares, and of always looking away or being in the toilet when it should have been her turn to spend money for group activities.

Whether life had made her like this or whether she had always been so was a problem that intrigued Nakajima.

Masuta-san's history was open to much speculation. She had been what is called an *oshikake nyōbō*, *nyōbō* being a bride and *oshikakeru* meaning to go uninvited or to force one's way in.

According to Nakajima there used to be a custom (apparently still followed on rare occasions) whereby if a man expressed his intention of marrying a girl and then unduly delayed the marriage, the girl would force herself on him by moving into his house with all her possessions. She would refuse to leave (and never give him the opportunity to throw her out) until they were married.

After its stormy origins Masuta-san's marriage had been a happy one for many years until her husband was killed in a plane crash. She had inherited his considerable wealth but from that moment had been unhappy. She had quarrelled with her children, now grown up, had become suspicious of sons-in-law and daughters-in-law, and had turned in upon herself. Then, in order to fill her empty days, she had begun teaching Japanese to foreigners. Even though she did not need the money, she always squeezed the last drop she could get from her pupils. She had become a hard woman and a lonely one.

It was because they knew she was lonely that Nakajima and the others put up with her. But the 'putting up' process generated a lot of resentment and Nakajima would sometimes spend twenty minutes or so blowing off steam to Andrew after such an encounter.

At this cold, bleak time at Kawaguchiko during the season off, events took an unexpected turn.

It was the second and last night of their stay and they had gone into the town after dinner to see a traditional Japanese dance which, unusually for the time of year, was being performed by a travelling troupe. Masuta-san had been more than ordinarily stingy during that day and had somehow avoided paying her share of the taxi fare from the hotel. So when the dance was over, instead of the six of them taking two taxis, Nakajima and the other four, all chattering and giggling and making small talk to cover their action, piled into one taxi, leaving Masuta-san to call another one for herself.

They felt guilty doing it and it was indeed against their natures. When they arrived at the hotel a few minutes later, they went quickly to their rooms without waiting for Masuta-san.

## SEASON OFF

The next morning after breakfast they all assembled downstairs in the lobby of the hotel, bags packed and ready to leave for the station. But Masuta-san was late. After a while they went to her room. It was empty. They enquired whether she had eaten breakfast downstairs. She had not.

They looked at each other, these venerable ladies in their kimonos, and they were suddenly afraid.

The season off at Kawaguchiko is indeed bleak. At night, especially a moonless one, the road beside the lake is dark for much of the way. There is ice at the lake's edge and frozen rain in puddles and the hotel lights seem warm between the pine trees.

They found Masuta-san at the bottom of a slope below the road. She had a broken hip and had frozen to death.

She had decided to walk home.

# 9
# THE FLOWERS OF THE FLOATING WORLD

Anyone who has ever bought a *ukiyoe* print has come into contact with the Floating World, albeit perhaps unwittingly. These pictures of actresses, courtesans, scenes of the Yoshiwara entertainment district, et al., are reproduced by the million and are as symbolic of Japan to the Western eye as Mount Fuji and cherry blossoms.

As Nakajima, who delighted in explaining the origin of words, told Andrew, *uki* comes from the verb to float, the Chinese character for *yo* means the world or society and that for *e* signifies a picture.

The Floating World flourished during the Genroku period of the late seventeenth and early eighteenth centuries and has survived, with alterations of style and form but largely unchanged in its basic function of providing entertainment, pleasure and escape, as the present-day *mizu shōbai*, or water business. Both expressions imply fluidity and impermanence, important features of the night-life of the entertainment quarters.

Whereas the heroines of the old Floating World were the geisha, the courtesans and other entertainers, those of the *mizu shōbai* are the hostesses. There are still geisha, of course, but their numbers have been decreasing steadily due to the alternative forms of employment and a reluctance to submit to the years of training necessary for the formation of an artist as skilled in music and dance as the true geisha must be.

The ranks of the hostesses, on the other hand, continue to be filled by young girls, and number probably hundreds of thousands throughout Japan. Their function is also to entertain, to please customers and to encourage them to spend their money, but their cultural achievements vary from individual to individual and their training is negligible.

\* \* \*

Not far from where Andrew lived in Roppongi there was a piano bar in the basement of a building. If he stopped the taxi at the Roppongi crossroads and walked home down the hill, he passed it on the way. It was often a temptation to go inside, a temptation he usually resisted. When he did go in, however, he always found a peculiar enchantment there.

It was a late-night place, open until nearly dawn, and in the early hours of the morning there was an air of unreality and timelessness, as if those hours had assumed diminished importance but elongated duration.

The most fascinating people would be seen at the piano bar, either perched on stools around the white grand piano or sitting at the small tables nearby. Andrew wondered whether they really were fascinating or whether in his tiredness they simply appeared to be so. These people in the piano bar were, he thought, the flowers of the floating world, some of them faded, some still radiant, but all of them about to be put away for the night.

There they sat, resting from whatever their labours had been, listening to the music, talking in a desultory way, and merely postponing the end of the night.

One person who was often seen at the piano bar was a young woman with the professional name of Mimi. Andrew knew her because she was a hostess at the Chinatown Cabaret, a place he frequented. In her job there she wore a long Chinese robe with a high collar, long sleeves and the skirt slit to the hips. In that guise she appeared small and slight but, when she came to the piano bar after work, wearing more severe clothing, like tailored suits, it was clear she was in fact robust and solidly built.

She was an attractive girl with regular features, large, doe-shaped eyes and black hair falling to her waist. She smiled only occasionally, and seemed very serious and preoccupied. She was always waiting for someone. Waiting takes up a lot of time in the floating world.

Whenever Andrew saw Mimi at the piano bar he was just about to tear himself away from his inertia to leave, so had not as yet come across the person she was waiting for. On one occasion, however, that person arrived before Andrew left and they were introduced with due formality. The name of Mimi's friend was Fujiko.

Mimi and Fujiko seemed extremely absorbed in each other. Andrew noticed at one moment that Mimi was holding Fujiko's hand under the bar, as one might hold the hand of a lover. He wondered whether their relationship was more than platonic.

Mimi said that they shared an apartment in Yotsuya, two rooms with kitchen and bathroom. At that moment Mimi's younger sister was also there. She had come from Kyushu for a week or two and, Mimi said, was acting as a secretary to both of them, taking telephone calls at night. If they were indeed a couple, it would be Mimi who played the leading role.

Fujiko was just nineteen years of age. When she went to the powder room, Mimi turned quickly to Andrew and started talking to him about her. She came, Mimi said, from a very traditional family in the country. They were wealthy but careful with their money and tried to keep Fujiko on a limited allowance. She was in Tokyo to study dress-designing but had to supplement her allowance by working part-time as a hostess in a bar in Roppongi, not far down the same street as the piano bar and close to Andrew's apartment. At that point Fujiko came back and Andrew bid them both goodnight.

A few days later Andrew was surprised to receive a telephone call from Mimi. She talked about Fujiko and said that they had discussed Andrew a lot since their last meeting. Fujiko wanted to learn English, as it would be useful to her in the dress-designing business. When she had finished her studies in fashion in about three years' time, she and Mimi intended to leave the floating world and set up a small fashion-design business together. Would Andrew be willing to give her regular English lessons? Fujiko could not afford to pay for them just now but she found Andrew very attractive and she, Mimi, wanted to offer him Fujiko in return for the lessons.

Warming to her subject, she went on to extol the virtues of

her young friend: her gentleness, her good heart, her healthy body and the affection she had felt for Andrew from their first meeting. She suggested Andrew take Fujiko out that evening. He could take her anywhere and she would follow him wherever he wanted to go and do whatever he wanted to do. This sentence was followed by a pause and '*Anata wa otoko desu kara, yoku wakarimasu ne*' (you are a man and so you understand very well what I mean, don't you?).

Andrew and Fujiko met for dinner at a rooftop restaurant in Shibuya called the Twilight. (The particularity of this restaurant being that it was possible to reserve a room for the night at the same time as booking the table. The bill for the whole operation was presented on departure.) The dinner gave them the chance to talk together without Mimi. Andrew was intrigued by Mimi's proposition but wanted to find out more about Fujiko before accepting it.

He found Fujiko to be an intelligent person and her desire to learn English seemed to be genuine. The first words she uttered under his instruction had an accent which he thought irresistible. She was so young at nineteen, twelve years younger than he, that he hesitated at first but finally fell under the same sort of spell as that which always drew him to the piano bar.

After dinner they took the lift to one of the lower floors where their room had been reserved for the next few hours. It was a Japanese-style room with the usual comforts, and the double futon had been laid not in the main room or in an alcove but in a connecting second room. This was tiny, not much bigger than the futon itself.

In the bath they washed each other and kissed, standing at first until, under Andrew's soapy caresses, Fujiko began to tremble. On the futon she was shaken by orgasm after orgasm. In one such moment her foot hit the wall beside the futon and a panel slid back to reveal a mirror. When they tried the other walls, they found the same thing. There were mirrors on three sides of the room, all at the level of the futon.

Fujiko's whole body was responsive to caresses. Although

very young, it was clear to Andrew that she must already have had a wide experience of love. Caressing her was like turning over the pages of a much-read book.

There was, however, a puzzling dichotomy in her behaviour. In spite of the intensity of her responses, her affectionate cooperation and her tenderness, she was passive. She was like a beautiful instrument to be played. Andrew wondered if this explained Mimi's offer of her to him, as if she were Mimi's property to be given to a friend for his enjoyment.

After the first phase of their lovemaking they paused to rest and take another bath. Fujiko had to telephone Mimi to say that she would be late—she was supposed to meet Mimi at the piano bar soon after midnight and it was now nearly twelve. She had to make three telephone calls to different places before she located Mimi at the Almond *kissaten* (coffee shop) at Roppongi. Fujiko was kneeling, naked, on the tatami, as she spoke to Mimi, and the conversation was interrupted by laughter and kisses. Mimi must have had difficulty understanding what she said, because Fujiko had to explain. *'Kisu shiteru'* (we're kissing), she said, giggling into the telephone. She agreed to meet Mimi at the piano bar at 1.30 a.m.

An hour later they had a third and final bath. They were happy and tender towards each other. Although Fujiko had drunk nothing all evening, not even at dinner, she was so tired she looked drugged. Andrew dried her and helped her dress. She took what seemed to be an eternity to put on her make-up. She had a collection of lipsticks in all colours, even a white one. Andrew, mystified, sat and watched her.

It was a week before they met again and the events that followed enlightened Andrew as to the nature of Mimi's relationship with Fujiko. Mimi had telephoned him and prevailed upon him to take Fujiko and her to dinner. They were both very hungry and ate as if they had not eaten for a week. Mimi said that she had been too busy to cook.

When dinner was over, it was nearly 10 p.m. and Mimi said

that Fujiko was on duty at the bar where she was an *arbeiter*, or part-time worker.

'It is a very amusing place,' Mimi said. 'I found the job for Fujiko there myself. It's quite close to where you live, as I told you. Let's go there together. Fujiko will do her job and you and I will be customers.'

When they entered, the lights were subdued and at first it seemed indistinguishable from thousands of other places. They were soon joined at their table by a hostess and Fujiko, who had changed into a kimono.

'Don't you notice anything, Andrew-chan?' asked Mimi.

'Nothing in particular.'

'Look at the barmen over there. Don't you see anything unusual about them?'

'They're very good-looking, I must say, and very smart. Also they're smaller than most barmen.'

'They're not men, Andrew-chan, that's why. They're girls and the hostesses are sometimes not girls but boys. This place has been christened the Supermarket. There are sister-boys and brother-girls and ordinary boys and ordinary girls, all the four sexes. The owner says you can take your pick, like in a supermarket. What do you think of our two hostesses?'

'Beautiful, but Fujiko is not a boy, I can assure you.'

'What about the other one, the one sitting beside me?'

Andrew looked at the hostess who had fine features but was otherwise camouflaged by her kimono. He could only guess.

'There is only one way to find out for sure,' Mimi said.

'Yes, I know, but I'd rather not risk it. Why don't *you* find out?'

Mimi gave one of her rare smiles and, amid giggles from the hostess, her hand disappeared into the folds of the kimono.

'Mimi, *yamete!*' Fujiko said sharply. (Stop that!)

Mimi looked up, surprised.

'You promised, Mimi. You said never again.' Fujiko's eyes were flashing.

'I know I did, but this is just a game.'

'If it's a game, let Andrew-chan play it. You know what you promised me.' Tears had welled up in her eyes and began rolling down her cheeks.

Mimi left her seat and moved over to sit beside Fujiko. She put her arm around Fujiko's shoulders and Fujiko clung to her. Soon Fujiko stopped crying and looked up cheerfully at Andrew and the other hostess, as if nothing had happened. But she still clutched Mimi's hand and Mimi's arm was still around her.

The brief squall had blown over. Mimi and Fujiko sat side by side like two lovely flowers on a single branch. Andrew looked from one to the other in fascination. There they are, he thought, **the** flowers of the floating world.

# 10
# GIRI-MAN

When Andrew first heard the expression *'giri-man'* uttered amidst uproarious laughter by a senior Japanese banker at a fairly drunken party, he could not persuade any of those present to explain what it meant.

He questioned Nakajima about it, but she put her fan across her face, so that only her cunning old eyes were visible, and he was not sure if the fan concealed a smile or if she was as horrified as she pretended to be.

'*Saa!*' she exclaimed. 'Where did Paton-san hear such a *warui kotoba* [bad word]?'

'It was the president of a large Japanese bank who used the word. I know roughly what "giri" means but what about "man"?'

'Let me hear what you think giri means, Paton-san.'

'Ah, sensei, I feel great trepidation in trying to define it to a Japanese, but here goes! As I understand it, "giri" is a duty that one performs reluctantly, painfully, and with a touch of resentment. It is not something one does with love. It is like the things one does for the family of one's in-laws.'

'That is very good, Paton-san.'

'Thank you, sensei. But what can the phrase "giri-man" mean?'

'It is already late and I must go now. Please forgive me; there are words I do not know, even in Japanese, and if I did know them, I could not let them pass my lips, Paton-san. That sort of warui kotoba need not be taught to gaijin-sama. Paton-san is not married, anyway. *Dōmo sumimasen*, Paton-san. *Ja, sayonara, sayonara.*'

She spoke the last two words, bowing twice and walking a few steps backwards, before turning and opening the door. From the outer office she bowed once again.

'*Sayonara*, Paton-san, *ki o tsukete, ne.*'

As she passed his secretary she said a few words to her in a low voice that Andrew could not hear. They both giggled.

Andrew continued to be intrigued by the phrase and wondered what not being married had to do with it. The mystery was eventually solved by a Japanese friend of his, a dentist whom he met occasionally at a basement beer-hall in Ginza Yon-chome called the Munich. The habitués of this beer-hall, which was the replica of a small German establishment in the city of Munich, had formed themselves into a club of which Andrew was the only gaijin member.

Obata-sensei, the dentist, was a jovial man in his fifties who spoke good English and who had obtained a doctorate in dentistry in America. Although he encouraged Andrew to speak Japanese, he would always revert to English if the conversation wandered into incomprehensible territory. Obata had a lively sense of humour.

'Giri-man?' he laughed. 'You don't have to worry about that. Probably you never will; it is more likely to occur in arranged marriages than in love matches.'

'Then there is a connection with marriage?'

'Oh yes. You see, "man" here is short for *o-manko*, one of the words for the female sexual apparatus. There are many other words as well, by the way, and also many words for the man's equipment. I'll write you out a list, if you like.'

'That would be interesting.'

'Yes, it's part of your education, Paton-san. I'll write the list out and give it to you next time I see you. Your sensei will never tell you these things.'

'You're quite right there. She said she could not let such words pass her lips.'

'Your sensei is a lady, Paton-san. Now you have guessed what giri-man means, haven't you? It means a man's duty to perform sexually with his wife when he doesn't love her or when he feels it is a duty he is obliged to fulfil or when he is simply too tired. I can tell you a true story about it if you like. You'd be surprised how many stories one hears as a dentist. Some of my patients treat me as a sort of father-confessor. Would you like to hear?'

'Very much indeed.'

'Then fill up the glasses again and we'll go and sit up at the end of the bar in the corner and I'll tell you.'

There were four characters in Obata-sensei's story: a rich middle-aged businessman from an old samurai family whom Obata called Ishida (to conceal his real name), Ishida's wife, Yukiko (snow child), Ishida's chauffeur, Takano, and Takano's twin sister, Mariko.

Takano was not an ordinary chauffeur. He and Mariko were both well educated and from a good family in the north of Japan where the old Ishida fiefdom had been situated in the feudal days before the Meiji Restoration of 1868. The Takano family, also a samurai family, had fallen on hard times and the rich businessman, Ishida, had taken young Takano into his service as a chauffeur, as a favour to him while he completed his studies.

The relationship was complicated by differences between their clans in the days of their forebears. Obata did not go into the details but implied that the complexities of interlocking family obligations between the Ishidas and the Takanos made for an uneasy peace.

Ishida's wife, Yukiko, was many years younger than her husband and was a beautiful woman. In Takano's eyes she was infinitely desirable and it was, therefore, an unpleasant shock to him when he overheard his master, Ishida, saying to a friend after a party that he had to go home early for the purpose of giri-man.

It was indeed rare for Ishida to be so conscientious about going home; he would normally take a hostess, or sometimes a geisha friend, to one or other of the many love-hotels in Tokyo before returning to his own house. During these intervals Takano would sit and wait in the car with the engine running, so that the car-heater in winter or the air-conditioner in summer made it comfortable enough for him to study by the interior lights.

Young Takano became more outraged every time he thought

of Ishida's remark and perhaps it was an ancestral ghost that prompted him to avenge it.

His twin sister, Mariko, worked as a masseuse for one of the agencies catering for the respectable end of the massage business, and occasionally Yukiko called her to her house for a massage before sleep. On one such occasion, Takano, recognising an opportunity to learn more about the Ishida ménage, dressed in his twin sister's clothing, applied a little of her make-up and came to massage Yukiko in her place.

This resulted in Yukiko's seduction, not so much because Takano actively tried to seduce her as because in the intimacy of the bedroom Yukiko confided in what she assumed to be a woman. She told Takano that she was lonely and in her heart of hearts longed for a man's embrace—a situation that Takano could hardly have been expected to resist. He declared himself and was accepted. It was a union made in heaven.

From then on Yukiko called for a massage with increasing frequency and, as long as his duties permitted it, Takano came, dressed as his sister. Moreover, as he was busy on most nights, Yukiko found that massage was really more beneficial in the daytime during the hours when Ishida had no need of his chauffeur.

Takano worshipped every part of Yukiko's body, and that part to which her husband had referred as the object of an unwilling duty Takano treated with the reverence due to a shrine, and the love due to a thing of beauty and delight.

One night when Ishida was very drunk and Takano was driving him home, he made some reference to his wife, to which Takano replied with a polite and deferential but complimentary comment on Yukiko. For some reason this caused Ishida to let out a flood of home truths. Slumped in the back of the car like a drunken rag doll, he began by saying that Yukiko was a beautiful woman but the marriage had been an arranged one and he had never really wanted it. Furthermore, she still acted in bed like a semi-virgin. She was not interested in sex, Ishida said. He would like to have a son but so far she had never become pregnant.

He became maudlin. Yukiko had never made an effort to make

sex interesting and for him it had become giri-man. On the other hand the hostesses of the mizu shōbai invented games and elaborate variations for both his pleasure and theirs and were willing to explore and enact both his sexual fantasies and their own. He had always found them captivating and adventurous, whereas his wife offered him exactly what she had on their wedding night, with neither additions nor subtractions, and he had quite simply grown tired of it.

Why, he asked his chauffeur in an almost unintelligible slur, should he eat the same dinner for fifteen years when all over Tokyo there were suppers of far more appetising quality? His life, he said, was ebbing away and the process could be slowed down by adding spice and interest to his everyday activities. His interludes in the floating world spaced out the trivia and the boredom and coloured his whole existence with light and gaiety. To limit himself to his wife alone, with her uniform approach and her monotonous performance, was to abandon the world of pleasure and delight.

With that Ishida fell asleep. He had been talking to himself more than to his chauffeur and did not appear later on to have remembered a single word he had said.

One night soon after this, Takano's sister, Mariko, came to the house to massage Yukiko and to tell her that her brother had been sent to Osaka and Kyoto for a few days, driving some very important business visitors. Ishida himself had not accompanied the visitors and he returned unexpectedly just as Mariko was leaving. She was wearing her white masseuse's uniform and looked fresh and lovely. Yukiko had fallen asleep, the servants had gone to bed and had left Mariko to let herself out.

The house was very quiet. Ishida was sober and with a blend of wiles, charm and persuasion, added to a heavy dose of coercion derived from the ancient relationships between the Ishida and Takano families, not to mention the promise of a large sum of money, he managed to seduce Mariko.

They made love on cushions thrown on the tatami floor of

the room he used as a study. The encounter was even more successful than he had ever imagined it could be, and it must also have been much noisier than they had intended because it woke Yukiko from a deep sleep. She crept down the stairs on bare feet and walked silently towards the origin of the noise.

From a distance she had taken the sounds to be groans of agony and despair, followed by what seemed to be attenuated screams; and she half expected to find that someone, her husband perhaps, had been attacked by a burglar.

It was an old Japanese-style house in which the only rooms furnished in Western-style were the loungeroom and a formal dining room for guests. Ishida's study was enclosed by sliding shoji panels. Yukiko tiptoed towards it and slid open the shoji a fraction, so that she could peep in without being seen or heard.

What she saw amazed her. For one moment of horror she thought she saw her husband entwined with his chauffeur, Takano, so great was the likeness of the twin brother and sister. Less than a second later, however, she distinguished Mariko's female form in the faintly lit room and heaved a sigh of relief.

The couple were not looking in the direction of the shoji. In fact the struggle was now over and they had their eyes closed and were lying still. Yukiko did not want to endure the embarrassment of a confrontation, nor did she wish to hurt Mariko. She crept quietly into the study, picked up Ishida's trousers and left the room, leaving the shoji open behind her.

Later, when Ishida came upstairs to their bedroom, trouserless, she switched on the light and presented him with his missing garment. This was her moment of triumph.

There was a sequel to this story but Obata-sensei was not sure of its full ramifications. He knew that Yukiko had used the situation as a bargaining lever for certain advantages of a material nature but there were other things as well, he thought. On the material side he knew that Ishida had been persuaded to buy Yukiko a lovely little summer mansion in the pine-groves of Karuizawa, in the mountains not far from Tokyo. He seems also to have made some financial restitution to the Takano family, again relating to the complex and murky past of long ago. Takano ceased to be a chauffeur and was given the job of department head in Ishida's business and Mariko was able to buy a small business of her own.

It also appeared that the affair between Ishida and Mariko was still continuing, with Yukiko turning a blind eye to it.

For herself Yukiko was very happy. Over the years she was blessed with two children, handsome boys who looked very much like herself but with a trace of the Takano features, if one examined the resemblance closely.

Ishida himself was proud of them. They would carry his name into posterity.

# 11
# WINTER SNOWSTORM

Obata told a second story which he assured Andrew was based on real-life experience:

The Japanese gentleman sitting by the window in the First Class section of the plane was the epitome of wealth and sophistication. He looked as if he had been groomed, dressed and rehearsed for the part of an international tycoon. His clothes were American casual, expensively casual; instead of a tie he wore a choker; when he raised an arm to accept the magazine offered him by the stewardess, his cuff slipped back to reveal a heavy gold chain on his right wrist. On the left wrist he wore a large gold Rolex watch and on two fingers of the left hand and on one of the right he wore thick gold rings.

His longish hair was thick, grey-white in colour and coiffured with careful elegance. His face was smooth, as if the wrinkles had been ironed out. When he began to read the magazine, he put on thick-rimmed glasses which somehow completed the image. He was not the usual anonymous Japanese businessman dressed in a dark suit and tie and wrapped in the aura of a corporate image. He was a tycoon of a different sort, a tycoon of the cinema: a film director.

The American woman sitting beside him looked rumpled and untidy, although she too was expensively dressed. She illustrated the difference between casual and careless and was a good deal younger than the film director, probably in her early forties. Her features were good; she had a wide, attractive smile but her wrinkles were certainly not ironed out and she seemed to be at ease with them.

Her name was Sara Wolstonecraft; her profession, writer. She was travelling in her professional capacity with Hisao Horino, known in cinema circles as Teddy Horino. He had engaged her to rewrite the script of a film which he was to direct with English-speaking *nisei* (second generation) Japanese actors in Hawaii. This script had been rewritten twice before and Sara had a feeling that someone else would mutilate her version as well. It was a bone of contention between them.

'I don't know why everyone in the movie business thinks he can write better than the screenwriter,' she was saying. 'The first script written for this movie was perfectly all right. But the actors think they can improve on it, the director—that's you, Teddy—can't resist changing it, the producer probably thinks he can do it better still and the result is rewrite after rewrite. It costs a fortune and in the end the improvement is negligible.'

'Why should you care? You're being paid for it.'

'That's not the point. Writing words and phrases is not like baking cakes. Besides, I sometimes think that if I hadn't been lured into this business to prostitute my talents, I'd have time to write something really worthwhile.'

'That is your choice, Sara.'

'I know, damnit. It's my inability to resist the money, the fear of being poor again, that makes me judge myself.'

The plane was taking them from Kagoshima to Fukuoka, a comparatively short flight along the west coast of the island of Kyushu. A few minutes before, the sky had been clear and the flat green sea could be seen far below. Now suddenly a rocking, jerking, bouncing movement began and the Captain's voice came over the intercom, quiet, reliable and reassuring, asking all passengers to fasten their seat belts. The jet, he said, was passing through some air turbulence; there was nothing to worry about; please remain calm.

The bouncing became more pronounced. The plane seemed to fall fifty feet every time. It was enough for Teddy's briefcase, on the floor in front of his seat, to jerk his knees upwards, sharply and uncomfortably; enough for all the coats, blankets and pillows to be thrown around the cabin; enough for some other passengers to be noisily sick.

Teddy folded a blanket around him, closed his eyes and watched, like an alter-ego, his own reactions. He could no more stop observing his reactions than he could stop breathing. And yet he sometimes felt that this habit of detachment deprived him of playing a real role in life. It was, he thought, a professional hazard. In a sense, all of life is cinematographic, all the human emotions can be sharpened to dramatic intensity, all situations can produce two reactions: the real-life one and the film-life one. This was Teddy's dilemma; he existed so much in the film-life that he suspected his real-life of being a tinsel copy of the imaginary. Thus he found himself examining his own spontaneous reactions to situations through the quizzical eye of his cinema other-self. He found himself qualifying even his most natural reactions as overdone or melodramatic.

He sat quietly in his seat, eyes closed, and waited to feel real fear, real panic. He felt nothing.

'Are you asleep, Teddy?' Sara asked. 'And if so, how can you sleep at a time like this?'

'No, I'm contemplating. Have you heard of detachment?'

'Of course I have. But how can you be detached just now? I feel I'm about to be detached from everything, from the plane, from the planet.'

'I mean spiritual detachment.'

'Who needs that, when the other is about to happen?'

'You do, Sara, you need spiritual detachment, to see things in perspective, as they really are.'

'The perspective from here is 30 000 feet and likely to reduce rapidly.'

The Captain's voice came once again over the intercom. He was speaking steadily in a measured and masculine way.

'Due to bad weather conditions at Fukuoka we will be unable to land for twenty minutes or so. We very much regret this delay and apologise to passengers for the inconvenience.'

A stewardess who had gone to the aid of a sick passenger was suddenly thrown off balance and fell down the aisle beside Sara.

Teddy wondered how the weather conditions could be expected to improve in twenty minutes. Looking out the window he could see nothing but a grey-white fog. Perhaps they were in a snowstorm. It was, after all, the middle of winter.

Only yesterday they had flown above the Japan Inland Sea from Osaka to Kagoshima and it had been a clear, beautiful day. Below them the sea had been a deep, transparent green, clear seemingly to the bottom. Here and there there had been parallel traceries of ships and boats, small pointed things followed by a white wash as the sea was disturbed by their intrusion. Sometimes they had glimpsed what appeared to be sunken islands or deep coral reefs but these were only the dark reflections of scattered clouds hanging above the glittering water.

The bumping and jerking seemed worse now. For the first time Teddy felt a cold fear slip into his stomach. He did not look at Sara to see what her reaction was. He closed his eyes, put his hands on his stomach, where the fear was, and waited.

'Teddy, are you still there?' It was Sara's voice from a long way off.

'Yes, Sara?'

'Aren't you scared, Teddy?'

'Of course I'm scared.'

'Thank God for that, at least. I was afraid you had turned into an imperturbable Buddha. What would you miss most if the plane never did land?'

'Love.'

'I need hardly have asked. Your reputation is quite awful, you know. Are you as bad as they say?'

Teddy opened his eyes and rose to take the bait. 'I am a very discriminating person, Sara, and my love affairs have been works of art. Do you remember the film we saw on the plane recently, *Modesty Blaise*?'

'Yes.'

'Do you remember where the Scottish accountant, McWhirter I think his name was, who was perpetually obsessed by money, complains that Gabriel spent 36 000 dollars on sex in a month and Gabriel, Dirk Bogarde, replies superbly, "Some people have quite the wrong idea of the value of money."? I thought that was wonderful.'

'Do you spend so much on sex?'

'Of course not, but I was thinking that what has furnished my life with its finest and happiest memories is love. Of all the things I have ever spent money on, love is the only thing I can remember when I realise that it is just possible I may die in the next half-hour.'

'Do you mean love or sex, Teddy?'

'In my experience the difference has been one only of duration. What would *you* miss most of all if the plane did not land?'

'I think I'd miss not ever having written the book I really want to write, my pagan hymn to the joy of life. I would want to finish it, even if it were never published but merely stored away to be found by someone in the distant future who would understand it and raise his eyes joyfully to God.'

'I didn't know you were religious, Sara.'

'I'm not. I can't explain it and there's probably not much time to analyse it, anyway, but it's there.'

They were silent.

Teddy closed his eyes again. The fear in his stomach settled and became almost dormant. The world closed in on him behind his eyelids and he thought—not as a puppet of the cinema, but as himself. He thought and found himself reliving those parts of his life that had been the most real and the most memorable. What he had said to Sara had been true. Each incident and person he recalled had been in the context of love. He tried to concentrate on something else, his houses, his books, his money, but they all disappeared again, refusing to be the subject of his dreams.

The plane suddenly fell sharply and the seat belt jerked into his diaphragm. Just as suddenly it rose again. Personal possessions were scattered everywhere. One of the stewardesses wore an expression of stark terror and a woman not far from them screamed.

Teddy opened his eyes and looked at Sara. 'Do you want

a hand to hold on to, Sara?'

'Yes, very much.' She took his hand. The plane gave a sickening lurch and her grip tightened.

'Jesus, Teddy, I'm scared to death!'

There was another lurch and with her other hand she grasped his arm, clinging to it, burying her head in his shoulder, her lower body constrained by the seat belt. He could feel her shudder. The plane steadied itself and, after a moment, she relaxed, smiled wanly and straightened up.

'Hell's bells, I thought that was it! Teddy, if we get out of this alive, let's do something spectacular.'

They had known each other for many years and had a good working relationship, but there had never been anything personal between them. Sara thought of him as a playboy. He thought of her as a workaholic. These superficial labels had simplified and limited their knowledge of each other.

'What could we do, Sara?'

'We could, for example, take a two-week holiday together in Hawaii.'

'You mean romantic?'

'If you like, but I always thought you considered me to be a frump.'

'What's a frump?'

'It's what you think I am. An untidy mess of a woman.'

'Aren't you though?'

'No, not really, that's my professional persona, that's what people expect me to be in this business. When I first started screenwriting, nobody took me seriously, they just wanted to get me into bed.'

'What are you then in private?'

'I'm a woman.'

She smiled at him almost shyly.

'And what have you thought of me all these years, Sara?'

'Oh you, Teddy. You've been the typical playboy, a member of the male conspiracy to screw every woman in the film business.'

'Then why would you take a romantic holiday with me?'

'Because underneath it all I don't think you're as callous as I thought. The question looks like being of academic interest anyway, the way things are going. I wonder what would happen if we *did* spend two romantic weeks on one of the quieter islands in Hawaii.'

'Who knows, Sara, we may live happily ever after.'

'Like in the movies?'

'Like in the movies.'

The plane was banking, losing height and banking again, coming lower and lower. This time it was the voice of a stewardess which announced that within a few minutes they would be landing at Fukuoka airport.

Teddy looked out of the window. There was nothing to be seen but grey cloud. Down and down came the plane and still there was no visibility. Then, only a few feet from the ground, or so it seemed, he saw a line of lights on the snow-covered runway. There was a bump, bump and the plane had landed.

That night they were taken by their Japanese hosts to a traditional geisha party. They sat cross-legged on the tatami floor and drank numerous small cupfuls of sake poured out for them with due ceremony by the geisha. They observed the patterns of parallels and perpendiculars formed by the borders of the tatami mats, the sliding shoji and the panelling of the walls and ceiling—an ensemble that produced an effect of peace.

The geisha danced to the twang of the samisen and played childish games. Soon it was 9 p.m. and the party was drawing to a close. They were warm with the sake and soothed by the atmosphere of otherworldliness and make believe with which the geisha had surrounded them.

Teddy had not been sitting near Sara and at this informal, final stage of the party he walked around to where she was sitting, squatted on his knees in front of her and offered his sake cup to her with both hands. She accepted it and he filled it for her. She toasted him, and drank. Then she returned the cup to him and filled it. '*Kanpai*,' he toasted, and emptied it.

'Did you mean it about a holiday in Hawaii?' he asked.
'Yes, of course. Did you?'
'Yes, I did. Are you ready?'
'To leave the party, you mean?'
'I mean to go to Hawaii. We'll leave tomorrow morning, as early as possible. If we have only a very faint chance of living happily ever after, the sooner we find it out the better.'
'Teddy, what about the film and the screenplay?'
'You can finish it after the holiday. It's only a film, after all.'
'Are you serious about holding up the schedule for two whole weeks? You've never done anything like that before. The schedule has always been sacred.'
'Yes, so sacred that I've had the screenplay written three times! Who have I been kidding? You said yourself that the first script was good.'
'I know I did but you've never taken any notice of anything I've said before. Okay, I'll be ready to leave tomorrow morning, Teddy. I think it's going to be a marvellous adventure. I really do have a wonderful feeling about it, but I still can't understand how you, of all people, can hold up the schedule for two weeks.'
'Look at it this way, Sara. How much longer would the schedule have been held up if the plane had crashed?'

Andrew was curious about the sequel to this adventure. If, as Obata had said, it was true to life, he must surely know what happened after the two weeks in Hawaii. But he seemed reluctant to elaborate.

'You don't like my story, Paton-san?'
'Yes, I do. I think it's most exciting, but the ending seems indefinite. You *do* know what happened, don't you?'
'Yes, but if I tell you, you will see that I have actually lied to you. You see, the events and the feelings are absolutely true, especially the feelings of the Japanese man; but I have disguised both the characters. For example, he was not a film director. He was a dentist.'

Light began to dawn.
'And what was the American woman—Sara?'
'Sara was not her real name but she was indeed a scriptwriter. Now she has become a novelist. She is also my wife.'

# 12
# THE CHAMPS ELYSÉES OF TOKYO

The café Champs Elysées has long since gone, bulldozed away to make space for new construction in a changing city. It used to be almost next door to the Hotel New Japan on the main road between Tora no Mon (the Gate of the Tiger) and Akasaka Mitsuke, and stood on the lower side of the road facing the Akasaka entertainment quarter. It was a low, one-storey building (an uneconomic use of valuable land); a wide, inviting café such as one finds on the Champs Elysées in Paris. It had been aptly named.

People came there to meet other people, either by appointment or by general design, because it was well known as a place where young ladies anxious to make rapid friendships would sit over an empty cup of coffee and smile brightly at a promising man at another table. One of Andrew's friends had been smiled at in this way just as he entered and, when he smiled back, the girl had leapt to her feet, come to the door and called a taxi for both of them before he knew what had happened. They had gone to a small hotel in Shibuya and a beautiful romance had begun.

The young ladies who frequented the Champs Elysées were never professionals. They were models and actresses who needed occasional help with their financial commitments. They were almost always very good-looking and well dressed; it must have been management policy to turn away female customers who did not come up to the required standard.

The story that centred around the Champs Elysées was again one which Andrew was able to piece together slowly from Nakajima's gossip and from a little of his own investigation:

Among Nakajima's many students was a Canadian couple by the name of Hackett. Arnold Hackett was a senior executive of an American oil company, and his wife, Ann, occupied her free time (which was *all* her time) in social activities, flower arranging and painting classes. For the mundane affairs of life she employed a cook, a gardener and two maids.

Usually the Hacketts had joint lessons with Nakajima. They were enthusiastic but unpromising students, since they were always too busy to study, and their progress through the textbook was painfully slow. Nakajima encouraged them but was resigned to the situation, the redeeming aspect of which was the fact that the American oil company paid her generously and regularly, whether the Hacketts had their lessons or skipped them to go out.

One day Nakajima asked Andrew to alter the day of one of his lessons. The reason for doing this was that the Hacketts were not speaking to each other and had henceforth to be taught separately. This had set in train a whole series of changes in Nakajima's schedule, involving six or seven of her students of whom Andrew was the last to be affected, even though his lessons took place at lunchtime and those of the Hacketts took place in the evening.

Nakajima was most apologetic. '*Dōmo sumimasen deskedo ne.* I didn't want to trouble you but you always help me. Paton-san *wa ü hito, desu ne, to*temo.'

Andrew looked into her conniving old face and asked how changes in evening lessons could impinge on daytime ones. It was a rhetorical question, long experience having taught him that he could never expect her to give the real reason for anything.

However, when asked why Arnold and Ann Hackett, whom he knew quite well, had ceased talking to each other, Nakajima's face lit up with interest.

'It's a *sankaku kankei*,' she said gleefully. (A love triangle.)

It had all started at Mano's Restaurant next to the rear door of the Copacabana nightclub in the crowded streets of Akasaka. Ann had been to dinner with some friends on one of the many nights when Arnold had been obliged (in the strict course of duty, of course) to spend the evening with a group of Japanese associates.

Mano's was a good place to dine. It was then managed by a short, fat gentleman with a black moustache and the air of a South American bandit. The chefs were said to be Russian. The dining areas were on different floors, joined by a very narrow staircase. The good food, very reasonably priced, and the bustling atmosphere of the place attracted a variety of customers. Some of these clients, usually female but occasionally of more ambiguous sex, would repeatedly leave their tables to hover on the staircase to make brushing acquaintance with other guests who had to squeeze past them. These moments of fleeting contact provided opportunities for propositions of more intimate encounters to be made and either accepted or declined.

It was while Ann and her party were drinking cognac after their dinner that James, the husband of one of the women present, mentioned this interesting aspect of Mano's and drew the attention of the others to what seemed to be taking place on the stairs.

'It's a wonder the waiters and waitresses don't complain about the obstruction,' Ann said. 'Look, that waiter almost lost his whole tray of food when the girl in the long black skirt stepped back from talking to that man.'

'I suppose they're paid danger money,' someone said, 'although that girl in the long black skirt is not a girl.'

'How do you know?'

'I've seen her here before. Mano's doesn't close till very late and the girl in the long black skirt develops quite a five o'clock shadow.'

'Is that true, James?'

'Yes, I can confirm it. I also heard of a customer who took her away in a taxi and had gone four or five miles before he discovered she was not a girl.'

'What did he do then?'

'He let her out of the taxi and went home alone. He said he didn't like girls with handles.'

'James, I do declare, you have brought us to a den of iniquity.'

'Not at all. The food is excellent, as you've all agreed, and it's not expensive, which is important, since I'm paying. What happens on the stairs is simply what happens on the stairs.'

'Like something that happened in the woodshed?'

'Yes, except that nobody ever knew what happened in the woodshed. Future generations of woodsheds will probably be equipped with television cameras and life's great unsolved mystery will be solved.'

'I always thought that the woodshed would be the last place on earth where I would like something to happen to me.'

'Then you should try the stairs, Ann. They are even carpeted and the corners there, between the floors, can't be seen from either above or below.'

'You should do something about James,' said Ann to James's wife.

'I've tried for years, darling, but he's quite incorrigible. I say, Ann, did you see who just went up the stairs then and practically bumped into the little girl in the tailored suit? It was old Smith, from James's office.'

'So it was,' said James. 'I can just make them out talking together where the stairs make a right turn. I suppose she is proposing celestial delights to him.'

'Surely he wouldn't accept them,' replied his wife. 'He's too old, don't you think so, Ann?'

'I'm not sure, dear. I've met him only once or twice. They do say that one underestimates the staying power of men of a certain age.'

'One does indeed,' said James. 'One always thinks that a person is old when he is ten or fifteen years older than oneself and the benchmark keeps getting higher every year.'

'Just look at that!' said Ann. 'Old Smith has been hooked; they're coming back down the stairs together.'

In fact old Smith came back, went to the coat-racks for his overcoat, while the girl in the tailored suit collected her own coat, and they walked down the lower staircase together.

'Well, I'll be blowed!' James said. 'It's a wonder he didn't see us looking at him.'

'Thank heavens he didn't, it would have been too embarrassing for words,' replied his wife.

'I'll tell you what,' said James, 'now that we have borne witness to this act of moral turpitude I'll take you all for a nightcap at a noisier place, where the same sort of thing happens. It's the Champs Elysées, just a few minutes' walk away.'

Outside it was a very cold winter's night. There had been a heavy snowfall the day before and the streets were still wet and sloshy, although most of the snow had either melted or been swept away during the day. The walk across to the Champs Elysées was brief but they were nevertheless glad to reach its warmth and find a table.

The café was crowded, music was playing somewhere, there was a hubbub of conversation and laughter and the crowd looked happy. Many of the patrons were young but there was a mixture of ages and types—mostly Japanese. It was after midnight and customers from the Akasaka cabarets were stopping here on their way home.

The waiter had just brought them a drink when James spotted someone on the other side of the café, near the other door to the street.

'I say, just look who we have here!' he said. 'Isn't that one Arnold Hackett, husband of one Ann Hackett, here present?'

Ann looked in the direction indicated.

'My God, it *is* Arnold!' she said. 'Why is he by himself? He was supposed to be with a crowd.'

'He probably came in for a beer. I'll go over and ask him to join us,' said James.

'Yes, please do that.'

James pushed back his chair to stand up and just as promptly sat down again. He was staring in embarrassed amazement. Ann was staring also.

Arnold Hackett had risen from his table a second before James had. He had put on his overcoat, wound his thick scarf around his neck and stepped forward to greet an attractive young Japanese woman who had apparently returned from collecting her fur coat from the cloakroom. She was a striking woman, very poised and elegant, and the thought flashed through Ann's mind that she looked exactly like something out of *Vogue* magazine.

Before anyone could react to the scene Arnold and the young woman walked, arm-in-arm, through the door and out onto the street.

Much, much later that night, when Arnold Hackett returned home and found Ann waiting up for him, he professed total innocence. Yes, he said, he had given a lift to the daughter of one of his Japanese colleagues, who had recently returned from modelling in New York. They had met accidentally when he was having a drink at the Champs Elysées and was reflecting quietly on the events of the evening before going home. Why had he then not arrived home until some three hours later? They had been talking, he explained, just talking. Nothing had happened, he assured his wife, nothing at all.

When the verbal battle had died down, Arnold said wearily, 'Look, Ann, I tell you nothing happened but I can't prove it. You'll just have to believe me.'

'You mean I'll never know for sure?'

'How can you? You just have to believe me.'

For several weeks after that night Ann Hackett refused to speak to Arnold and this was when their Japanese lessons were taken separately.

But she was to have her revenge.

The sumo wrestlers in Japan have great prestige and fame. Most them are mountains of men, extraordinarily powerful and extraordinarily fat. Their sport is of ancient origin and during the national championships at the Kokugikan at Kuramae in Tokyo the bouts are televised constantly and can be seen in every Japanese-style restaurant throughout the country. The champion sumo wrestlers are household names. Their photographs appear in all the newspapers and magazines. There can be no such thing as a sumo wrestler incognito.

Ann always enjoyed seeing the sumo bouts in the Kokugikan, where she had been several times with friends but never with Arnold. They would sit in a box, on cushions on the floor, eat Japanese food and drink sake and beer while watching the elaborate ceremony that led up to the bouts. Ann was fascinated by the ritual of the ring entry, the scattering of salt and then the silent tension the moment before the crash, when the human monoliths engage in terrible battle. The struggle is like the struggle of gods—brief, often all too brief, but decisive.

On one occasion a Japanese friend had arranged a little party at the end of the sumo season and Ann found herself face to face with some of the champions. One in particular, while still a huge hulk of a man, was not fat. He was good-looking and had something of a reputation as a woman-chaser. He had spent some time in America and spoke good English.

When Nakajima told Andrew about this meeting, she said that she felt sure that Hackett-san no okusan, that is, Ann, had been deeply impressed by her wrestler; more than impressed, in fact.

A few weeks later she brought Andrew a three-page cutting from a Japanese weekly magazine, given to scandal and erotica, and laid it on the table triumphantly.

'Look,' she said, 'I was right. Hackett-san no okusan has been away with him for the weekend.'

Andrew had difficulty translating the article at sight and would need many hours with his dictionary in order to do so. Nakajima therefore read it out to him. It described how Ann, with a group of women from a Tokyo painting class, had been to Ise for a weekend's painting and by coincidence Ann's friend, the sumo wrestler, had been staying by himself at the same hotel. The writer of the article had somehow found out that Ann had missed most of the painting excursions and had been escorted around the shrines by the sumo champion. There were three photographs of them together, one of them taken dancing in a nightclub.

One of the maids at the hotel also told the reporter that she had seen Ann coming out of the champion's room at five o'clock on the Sunday morning.

It was not long before Arnold Hackett was sent a translated copy of the article by the personnel manager of his company, with a request that he clarify the situation. The company, it appeared, was concerned with its image; and the impact of such an article, while perhaps not damaging, was, nevertheless, something the company did not need. It was hoped that the implications in the article constituted nothing more than scurrilous rumour-mongering without foundation.

Arnold was furious and the row that preceded the final declaration of peace in the Hackett ménage was said to have been momentous. Nakajima gathered evidence of this from both parties.

Ann assured Arnold that of course nothing had happened, except that the sumo champion, a charming man with great reverence for tradition and an amazing knowledge of history, had shown her around the temples and shrines at Ise and the surrounding area and had made them come alive for her.

As to the maid's story, that was nonsense. Obviously the journalist had either invented it or paid the girl to lie about it.

'However,' she concluded, 'you'll never know for sure, will you? So you'll just have to believe me. If you accept a truce on that basis, we'll call it quits.'

The following week Nakajima moved Andrew's lesson back to its normal day.

# 13
# THE HEAD OFFICE VISITOR

Kyushu is the southernmost island of Japan and perhaps the most beautiful. It gives the impression of always having been somewhat independent of and subtly different from the rest of Japan. It exerts a pull on the imagination, enhanced, of course, by the reputation of places like Beppu and Fukuoka as being uninhibited and fun-loving.

In Fukuoka there are large numbers of Japanese company employees who have left their wives and families back in Tokyo or Osaka while they do their stint in the Kyushu branch office. Moving house for a period of a year or so is too disruptive to the children's schooling and education of the young must be put before happy matrimony. Japan is a country where education and examinations are so fiercely competitive that there is an annual crop of adolescent breakdowns and suicides.

The old name for Fukuoka was Hakata and this name is still often used. A temporary bachelor is sometimes referred to as a *chonga* (a Korean word) and if he is in Hakata he becomes a Hakachon. With admirable consideration for the plight of the thousands of suffering Hakachons, the city of Fukuoka boasts more cabaret and nightclub hostesses per head of population than any other city in Japan. It can also be appreciated that when a company has dispatched its men to distant outposts, frequent visits by all levels of the hierarchy back in Tokyo are necessary to ensure that all is well. On each such occasion the local Hakachon feels obliged to entertain the visitor at his favourite bar or cabaret (at company expense, of course) and to make up the party he invites two or three members of the staff and business associates as appropriate. As this is reciprocated by both staff members and the outside contacts when they receive visits at their level, a really keen Hakachon may find himself in bars and cabarets nearly every night.

If he happens to be the local manager, he also has to contend with playing golf two or three times a week; and then there are lunches and business association meetings; weddings and funerals of staff and their relatives; showroom, shop and factory opening ceremonies; ship launchings and tours to be made to other parts of Kyushu. An executive may be said to have earned his spurs when finally recalled to the monolithic skyscrapers of Tokyo and the peak-hour underground scramble of those condemned forever to commute backwards and forwards between office and home.

The reputation of Kyushu has spread beyond the shores of Japan and there are some foreign visitors who feel that they, too, should see the problems of the region at first hand. One such gentleman was Hamilton Roff, a very important executive in the Sydney Head Office of Andrew's company, Radonics Ltd, which had a fifty/fifty joint venture with a Japanese enterprise in Kyushu.

Hamilton Roff was dynamic, demanding, bullying and tireless. He was fat, yet strangely agile; he had a complicated European mind which refused to simplify the really simple issues of life, with the result that he could keep his subordinates confused as to his wishes and then criticise them severely for their lack of intelligence and initiative in not doing what was required of them.

That Radonics Ltd had made reasonable profits in spite of the presence of Roff as one of its most senior managers is proof of the fact that some companies make money because they happen to be producing the right article at the right time, and not because of the brilliance of their day-to-day management.

A visit to Japan by Roff was always a dreaded event for the locally based European staff and sheer purgatory for the Japanese for whom the danger of misunderstanding his intentions was added to an already existing language barrier.

On this occasion, however, there was one particular point on which the desires of Hamilton Roff were unequivocal. He wanted to go to Nagasaki in Kyushu and he did not want to sleep alone. He transmitted this wish to Andrew who was to accompany him on his tour. Andrew advised the Japanese side of the joint venture company and he and Roff duly arrived in Nagasaki where they were to visit some shipyards and negotiate the sale of some Radonics equipment.

In the matter of amorous alliances it is no longer usual in Japan for girls to be provided, like cold beer or soap, for the use of guests. In less enlightened times this undoubtedly occurred and a host might have wished to make such a gesture to his guest in order to create an obligation of reciprocity. But today a free enterprise system prevails. The cabaret and bar hostesses are generally cooperative only if they like a man and have got to know him as a regular customer of the establishment. A gift of money then becomes a present, not the purchase price, and the girl does not lose her pride along with her virtue.

The request from Hamilton Roff that a girl be arranged for him rather threw the cat among the pigeons. Young Tanaka-san, the Nagasaki representative, was in a panic. In the first place, he had met Roff before and disliked him. And secondly, he did not know how to make sure that any girl would agree. He could see himself being adversely reported on to his superiors in the Japanese side of the joint venture and, even if they privately sympathised with him, they would publicly have to take some action, such as transferring him back to Tokyo.

This was what Tanaka feared most of all, because it happened that he was engaged in a passionate love affair with his secretary.

Nagasaki was possibly the least propitious place for the Roff enterprise. It is a splendid harbour city, picturesque and steeped in the history of early European and Japanese contacts. Some of the people even bear a resemblance to Europeans, transmitted from earlier contacts with the Dutch, the Portuguese and others. But although, like all Japanese towns, it has a flourishing entertainment industry, it is not a holiday resort like Beppu, nor a bachelor's paradise like Fukuoka. And the local girls are, if anything, more independent than elsewhere.

The night started with Hamilton Roff, Andrew and Tanaka at a sushi shop. Tanaka asked the owner for the big sake cups, not the usual small ones. Getting Roff drunk, he thought, would be an elegant way out of the problem. But he had mistaken his man. Roff was of the breed that alcohol only makes obnoxious and more determined than ever. Furthermore, his fat belly seemed to be a natural container for it. The sake just poured down and stayed there, as if it were a reserve tank.

The sushiya-san went on deftly moulding the small columns of rice in his hand, covering them with slices of raw fish and seafood and whisking them with a flourish onto the counter in front of the three men. Roff kept eating them as fast as they were put down, especially the expensive ones, like *uni* (sea urchin roe), *ō-toro* (the rich part of the tuna) and *odori* (dancing prawns, so called because they are alive and literally kicking). Tanaka kept on filling up Roff's sake cup and the whole lot—rice, fish, sake, sliced ginger and all—just slid noisily down into the bulging reserve tank.

After the sushi they went to a hostess bar. Tanaka hoped that this would short-cut the problem but unfortunately none of the girls found Roff attractive. They were unresponsive to both promises and bribes.

They then tried a nightclub. It was an expensive club, as befitted the guest's station, and furnished luxuriously. A Comba group was playing, the hostesses were in evening dress and looked beautiful. They also looked expensive and they were; but none of them cared to receive Hamilton Roff's contribution to her overheads.

During the process of negotiations Roff's reserve tank had been absorbing sake, then beer, then whisky and the only visible effect was a nasty glazing over of his eyes.

After the nightclub came a cabaret, a noisy place where they had no success.

At 1 a.m. they were in another bar. This one was a long way down the social scale, as bars go, but it had at last offered a glimmer of hope. They had been joined by two promising hostesses and Andrew was talking quietly to them, trying to make the necessary arrangements. Roff leaned over belligerently and tapped him on the shoulder.

'Andrew,' he said, 'I presume you have kept my instruction in mind?'

'But, of course, Hamilton. In fact, these ladies have just told me they are sleepy and would like to be taken home.'

Roff's eyes unglazed for a second and he rose agilely to his feet. The bar-owner called a taxi and Tanaka, exhausted and relieved, saw Roff, Andrew and the two girls drive away. He went back inside to have a cup of green tea.

The taxi headed out through the maze of narrow streets towards the hills above the city, where their hotel was situated, and it seemed as if the evening's efforts were about to be rewarded.

The evening had been a difficult one for both Andrew and Tanaka, but while Tanaka had escaped, Andrew had not. He had made what he thought was a sound, face-saving arrangement with the girls: they would both come to the hotel with the men, but only one would stay the night. This girl would be for Hamilton Roff and they could decide between them which one it would be.

When they arrived at the hotel, the girls said they needed to go home to change and would be back in a few minutes.

Roff did not like this turn of events, which certainly was unusual, and he said so. Andrew thought it might be a device by which they took the time necessary for deciding who did what. He soothed Roff's suspicions, saw him to his room, said goodnight and went to bed.

He fell instantly into a deep sleep. After what seemed like an eternity but was in reality only forty-five minutes, he was awakened by the telephone ringing.

It was Roff. Where, he wanted to know, was the girl? What was Andrew doing about it? Was this the way the company was run?

When Andrew's initial shock had passed and he had collected his wits, he reassured Roff that all would be well, it was still early, why not have a little sleep while he was waiting?

This produced a further explosion but Roff finally hung up.

Thirty minutes later the same thing occurred. Roff was

becoming more incoherent. Phone Tanaka, he screamed into the phone, I will not tolerate this inefficiency. Andrew said he did not know where Tanaka lived (which was a lie to protect his friend). A blast from Roff. *Why* did he not know where Tanaka lived? There are bad apples in this organisation that should be thrown out; he, Roff, would not be treated like this. The phone was slammed down. Silence.

Andrew, exhausted, fell asleep again. But not for long. Roff was back on the phone. It was 3.15 a.m. He was again on the phone at 3.45 and 4.30.

He had never been so insulted in his life, he said. Not only his honour but the very honour of Radonics Ltd was at stake. It was, he said, voice reaching for a higher key, an insult to Radonics.

After 4.30 there were no more calls. The great man's indomitable energy had faltered. He must have gone to sleep.

When they met at 9 a.m. in the foyer of the hotel, ready to start the visit to the shipyards with Tanaka-san, the atmosphere was glacial.

Hamilton Roff said only a few words and they were to the effect that the foreign shareholders would have to examine the staffing of the joint venture company more closely before putting any more money into it. Staff without breadth of vision or without an international outlook were hardly likely to measure up to the requirements of business in this modern world.

After his departure, Andrew and Tanaka, offering prayers to separate gods, half hoped that his plane would crash on its return flight to Sydney. Fortunately for their consciences, the deities were less indiscriminate in their carnage. Roff cut short a planned stopover in Hong Kong and arrived in Sydney three days earlier than he had originally planned.

He did not advise his wife of the change, however, and when he opened the door of his apartment in Sydney, it was to find that another man had been sharing it with her during his absence. In the fit of rage which this discovery provoked he suffered a heart attack.

The news came through that he would take early retirement on his release from hospital. His replacement would arrive in Japan during the following month to familiarise himself with Radonics' overseas operations.

As Andrew said to Nakajima at their next meeting, visitors from Head Office are one of the more serious hazards in the lives of expatriate and local executives alike.

# 14
# TOO MUCH HAPPY TIME

Nakajima spoke very little English but one phrase she would often use was 'too much happy time'. She would use it to sum up Andrew's explanation of a late party or a night spent in the entertainment quarters, or as an accusation when Andrew, short of sleep from the previous night, nodded off momentarily in the middle of a translation. In this case the phrase would be accompanied by an arch and indulgent smile.

Early one winter Andrew had to accompany an Australian from the Perth branch of Radonics Ltd to Hokkaido, the northern island of Japan. He took this man, whose name was George, to the hot spring resort of Noboribetsu for a weekend at the Grand Hotel. This was a large and luxurious hotel, equipped with an enormous bath-hall in which there were many pools and spas of different sizes and shapes, filled with water of varying temperatures, some sulphurous, some not. To George, seeing it for the first time, the bath-hall was an incredible sight. There was so much steam that an accurate estimate of its size was impossible to make but it gave the impression of being as large as an aircraft hangar. There were palms and foliage everywhere. The clouds of steam would sometimes move, lift, temporarily evaporate and then close in again, reducing visibility to a few feet. The largest pool, a Roman bath somewhere in the middle, was the size of a swimming pool and in fact some people managed to summon up the energy to swim a lap or two, as the water there was much cooler than in the smaller baths.

As always in public bath places, the bathers soaped and scrubbed themselves outside the bath and immersed themselves only when they were clean and rinsed free of soap. Then, if the water was very hot, they would ease themselves gingerly, inch by inch, into the scalding bath until they sat, absolutely still, with the water up to their necks.

The old habit of mixed bathing had disappeared in most parts of Japan, particularly in the cities, but in Hokkaido it was still practised and at the Noboribetsu Grand Hotel the clouds of steam were the only veils to protect modesty—that and the Japanese habit in public baths of walking around with a minuscule towel, called a *tenugi*, held in front of the sensitive area.

Finding himself in the same bath as unknown women was a new experience for George but it soon began to seem the most natural thing in the world. At one stage he was alone in the huge Roman bath when what must have been a busload of Japanese high-school girls, all in their late teens, jumped in from all sides at once and surrounded him, splashing and teasing him.

Taking a bath in Noboribetsu was not simply a once-a-day routine for cleansing purposes. It was the main object of coming to the hot spring resort and in bad weather, when outside activities were impossible, guests lived indoors for their entire stay. They would go to the bath-hall on arrival in the evening, spend an hour or more there, return to their Japanese-style room, drink beer or sake, have dinner brought to the room, return to the bath-hall before bed, have a massage, sleep, wake, go to the bath-hall before breakfast, and so on. The Grand Hotel also boasted an indoor golf driving range, a dance hall and other facilities.

When Andrew and George came out of the baths to dry, they wrapped themselves in towels and sat for a while in cane chairs, sweating profusely and relaxing from the enervating effects of the hot water. Andrew was telling George that, in his opinion, the much publicised Japanese attitude to nudity was less innocent and beguiling than was believed in the West, when his point was suddenly illustrated by three young women coming towards them. Each was shielded only by a tenugi. The first girl held hers across her pelvis, leaving the rest bare, the second concealed only her breasts, and the third, walking behind her two companions, held hers loosely in front of her. Then, as she drew level with the men, she whisked it away with a theatrical gesture and a mischievous smile.

On their first evening, after the baths and dinner, they donned the heavy *tanzen* (outer woollen kimonos) over their *yukata* (cotton kimonos) and went for a walk. At the door they had exchanged their indoor slippers for the high, wooden *geta*, or clogs, provided by the hotel for outdoor use. George had some difficulty walking on the geta at first, as they elevated his already tall frame by some four inches and it was easy for him to become unbalanced on their two wooden supports.

Outside in the cobbled street the air was pure and bracing but very cold. It was raining. They carried Grand Hotel umbrellas but soon decided that enough was enough and went into a bar. They sat on high stools at the counter near a smartly dressed young Japanese woman who was drinking by herself. Andrew smiled at her and asked her if she would care to join them. She accepted without hesitation. They introduced themselves and exchanged name cards. Her name was Watanabe Sumiko, profession: lawyer.

She spoke practically no English, so Andrew translated as best he could. George was obviously very attracted to Sumiko and kept plying her with questions, through Andrew.

She accepted a crème de menthe, then a whisky, then a brandy. She told them that she had already had four or five crème de menthes before they came. She wanted to talk, even if Andrew could not understand everything she said. She had had a good career in Osaka, she said, but recently she had been sick and had come to Noboribetsu for a few days' holiday. She was about thirty years of age and was poised, cultivated and beautiful.

In talking about her sickness she kept using a word ending in '-*byō*' (illness) but Andrew could not place the beginning of it. She seemed not to be unduly intoxicated by the constant stream of drinks. Andrew soon began to drink straight soda water with ice, having passed his quota. This he had measured by transferring a matchstick from one sleeve of his tanzen to the other every time his glass was refilled. Without this system he could not keep the score and concentrate on his interpreting at the same time.

George, however, had an amazing capacity for alcohol and

kept up with Sumiko, glass for glass. He confided to her, through Andrew, that he loved her. She accepted this touching declaration in the spirit in which it had been made and told him her room number at the Grand Hotel. The three of them left the bar together and walked back to the hotel. George and Sumiko took the lift together and Andrew found an excuse to miss it.

The next morning Andrew asked George if all had gone well.

'Absolutely nothing happened, old boy,' he replied. 'We went to her room together, we undressed, and the moment she sat on the bed she passed out. So I got dressed again and went to my own room.'

There was no word from Sumiko during the day. The hotel management said that she had gone out. After dinner that evening Andrew and George went once again to the same bar and found Sumiko there, drinking with two Japanese holiday-makers. She immediately excused herself from them and came to sit on a high stool at the bar between George and Andrew. She apologised to George for falling asleep the previous night and, to Andrew's surprise, suggested that she and George go back to the hotel now, before she drank too much.

This they did. George once again accompanied her to her room and Andrew went down to the bath-hall for another bath.

The next morning George reported to Andrew at breakfast that Sumiko had been wonderful. She had been almost desperately erotic, making love with a sort of burning physical passion, 'as if her life depended on it,' George said.

'Honestly, old boy,' he assured Andrew, 'she pushed me to my extremes and beyond. It went on and on and every time I felt I had to sleep she stirred me on again. I left her asleep at about two o'clock in the morning and went back to my own room. My God, what a girl! I tell you, Andrew, it was the experience of a lifetime. I think I could almost remain celibate for a year in homage to it.'

The day was fine and they went sightseeing to the Jigoku-Dani (the valley of hell), a ravine where from holes in the hillside pools of boiling mud bubble and splutter menacingly amid clouds of sulphurous steam. Andrew was taking a photograph when a messenger from the hotel arrived and asked them to return immediately. The police wanted to see them.

They found the police were questioning everyone who had been seen with Miss Watanabe Sumiko during the last forty-eight hours. She had been found dead in her bed by the maid at about 11 a.m. Beside her body there was an empty bottle of pills and an empty bottle of Scotch.

The barman from the bar where they had met Sumiko was there among the people to be questioned, as were three hostesses from the bar and the two Japanese holiday-makers whom Sumiko had left for George and Andrew the night before. One of them vented his spite at having been abandoned by telling the police that the two wicked gaijin had plied her with liquor in order to obtain her sexual favours. The bar hostesses did not know who she was, she was simply a customer, not a hostess, and she had appeared to have lots of money. She had tipped generously and had been nice to them. The barman said that the accusation that the gaijin had plied her with liquor was nonsense. The only drinks she had taken that night were provided by the two Japanese holiday-makers, who might very well themselves have had the intentions they ascribed to the gaijin. The hostesses supported the barman.

The following morning an autopsy was performed and it was found that Sumiko had been suffering from an inoperable terminal cancer. Further enquiries revealed that she knew this. Her doctor in Osaka had given her less than a month to live.

'The strange thing,' Andrew said to George, as they were boarding the plane from Sapporo to return to Tokyo, 'was that she didn't look sick. Tired, strained around the eyes, but not sick.'

George himself was shattered. This sequel to his night with Sumiko had been an unexpected shock. He did not know what he had thought might happen, whether, as he was married, their relationship could have had any future or not. A part of him had hoped that in some miraculous way it could have. But her death had come before even this remote possibility could be considered.

The next day was a Japanese lesson day and Nakajima was punctual. She entered Andrew's office with her usual greetings and bows and sat down in front of his desk.

She looked at him quizzically, noting his haggard appearance, and said, '*Ma*, Paton-san *wa tsukareta ne* (you're tired, aren't you)? Ja, too much happy time!'

# 15
# THE REAFFIRMATION OF LIFE

Claudius was a mid-European, urbane and cynical, whose work in Tokyo brought him into contact with Andrew. He had come to Japan alone, having recently been divorced. Why the divorce had taken place Andrew did not know and Claudius never spoke about it, but on the piano in his apartment in Harajuku stood a framed photograph of a young woman with two children, who Andrew assumed was the divorced wife.

Andrew later got to know Claudius quite well and would sometimes pick up this photograph and speculate on the story behind it. It is odd that the most traumatic events in the life of an individual can be reduced to the importance of a fleeting glance by those who were not involved. But when Claudius sat and played the piano, as he often did, it seemed to Andrew that his feelings flowed from him, wordlessly.

The girl in the photograph was beautiful in a tranquil way. Her eyes were far apart, her Nordic blonde hair long, her mouth wide. Above all she was composed and quiet.

Although Claudius never spoke about the events leading up to the divorce, he did one night tell Andrew how he had felt after it was all over. It had seemed to him, he said, that his life had stopped. The pain had gone, as if by surgery, but there was nothing to replace it. Thoughts that had filled his day from the moment of waking to the moment of sleeping were now swept away, leaving emptiness. From this emptiness of thought and feeling came a new awareness of the physical world around him and he sometimes found himself seeing objects, trees, birds, rocks, the sea, with shattering clarity, as if he had never seen them before and was for the first time a part of them and receptive to them. He was rediscovering life.

But even in this void of feeling he was needled by sexual desire. For a man in Claudius's position in Tokyo it was easy to satisfy the senses and he did so. However, he said, he found it strangely lonely to be going through the motions of love without love on either side, without memories, with nothing shared from the past. He felt more like an observer than a participant, and detached from much of the pleasure. He had a premonition that each facile experience would become more and more meaningless, until his heart became too dry and brittle ever to be able to love again.

One night he showed Andrew some photographs he had taken of himself and two geisha, using a Polaroid self-timing camera. These girls would often come and have a drink at his apartment, when they had finished entertaining at a party. His first affair had been with the elder one and then, at her suggestion, Andrew gathered, the younger one had been invited to join in. Andrew would have treated this as an idle story, or empty boasting, if he had not seen the photos of the three of them. But there they were, as large as life, performing gymnastics reminiscent of old Chinese erotica.

It was afterwards quite a shock for Andrew when he met these two geisha at business cocktail parties. They would take his glass to refill it and offer him small plates of food, oysters, slices of lobster or smoked salmon from the tables and, trying not to laugh at the incongruity of the situation, he would be seeing them in his mind's eye pursuing other activities in Claudius's apartment.

Then suddenly these adventures came to an end. Claudius said he was sick to death of the whole thing. He began to work very hard and told Andrew that he was leading an almost monastic life.

When Claudius went back to Europe on holiday at the end of the year, there was no news of him for nearly three months. In a hectically busy city like Tokyo, day slips quickly into day, week into week and month into month. There is not much sincerity in the social contacts one makes among foreigners. A hostess may give a dinner in honour of someone one day and hardly recognise him in the street two years later. These fragile social relationships are as short-lived as flowers. A similar idea has been expressed in a Japanese poem:

> *yo no naka wa*
> *mikka minu ma*
> *no sakura ka na,*

meaning that worldly things pass like the cherry blossom, and if you do not see it in its three days of flowering you will find it gone.

When Claudius returned to Japan after his holiday, Andrew found him completely transformed. He looked younger. His eyes shone, he radiated joy. He told Andrew that he had got married and invited him to come to his apartment for a drink and to meet his wife.

She was apparently in the bedroom combing her hair when he arrived and Andrew stood by the piano while Claudius poured the drinks. Then she came in.

If he had been holding a glass, he would have dropped it. Beside him on the piano was the photograph of the Nordic beauty he had so often admired and, coming into the room, smiling a wide smile, hand outstretched in welcome, was the same girl.

# 16
# THE FIVE-YEAR MARRIAGE CONTRACT

Nakajima had often told Andrew that in her view the ideal system of marriage would be one in which the union automatically ceased at the end of five years, allowing both parties to start again with a new partner for the succeeding five years. In her case she would have liked to try out different men, especially gaijin, without stepping beyond the accepted rules of marriage. Her main point was that she felt she should be able to choose, to refresh herself and her life, rather than accept a status quo.

As to the question of children under such an arrangement, she said that they should remain with the party best able to care for them. In any case she was a believer in minus-zero population growth, maintaining that this was a virtue in a world of profligate breeders. Her ideal system would be a kind of sequential monogamy.

In her spare time she made notes for a novel based on this idea. She never actually wrote it but she did write what would have been extracts from it, had it been completed. From time to time she gave Andrew these pages, written in her own hand, the Chinese characters and the connecting hiragana boldly and clearly drawn.

When he had worked on the notes and had understood them, they discussed them and Nakajima would embroider them and fill in the details of her story. The novel was to be divided into three parts, covering thirty years in the lives of a married couple. For the purpose of her novel she had compromised on the original idea of automatic divorce at the end of every five-year period, because this would be time-consuming and costly. Alas, she said, we do not live in an ideal world!

### THE CONTRACT    YEARS 1-5    TOGETHER

At the insistence of the wife in the novel, Michiko, a written contract was drawn up between her and her husband, Takeshi, setting out the rules as follows:

1. At the end of every five-year period each partner would be free. Takeshi would remain in his house in Yotsuya and Michiko would move out to her small aparto in Azabu.
2. This separation period would last for five years during which time either side could have affairs with other people. However, once every six months during this time they were to meet at the hot-spring resort of Atami and spend the weekend together in a love-hotel, specifically for sexual purposes.
3. At the end of the five-year separation period Michiko would return to Takeshi's house and live with him for the following five years, during which period each would be faithful to the other, any fall from grace to entail immediate divorce, final and irreparable.
4. They would have no children.

At the time of their marriage Michiko was a doctor with a small but growing practice in Azabu which she ran from her apartment there. She was twenty-five years of age. Takeshi, at thirty, was already a successful businessman. He was an ambitious, driving person, deeply involved with commercial affairs and his purpose in marrying had been to acquire a quiet, domesticated wife who would behave in the traditional manner. Unfortunately for him he had fallen in love with Michiko. Michiko, who was the projection of Nakajima herself in the novel, had also fallen in love with Takeshi but she refused to give up her medical practice and her independence and was determined not to marry unless the contract was signed on her terms. She won the day and it was to be a long time before she realised it was to prove a Pyrrhic victory.

### YEARS 5-10    SEPARATION

Nakajima's novel really began with the first separation period.

By this time Michiko was thirty and Takeshi thirty-five. Andrew was given an extract to translate and he discussed it with the author.

'Why, sensei,' he asked, 'is Michiko so happy to be free again, when you say she still loves Takeshi?'

'Because, Paton-san, she wants to taste other men as well.'

'She has no regrets in leaving Takeshi?'

'None at all. She is very happy. She likes to go skiing in the mountains. Her medical practice is thriving. She is at home in her little aparto in Azabu. She can come home at three o'clock in the morning if she likes and go abroad on holiday without asking anyone. Also she wants to taste a gaijin and she meets a visiting American professor at one of the universities in Tokyo. The American also likes to ski. They have a wonderful love affair.'

'And what happens if she wants to stay with him at the end of the five years?'

'She doesn't. The American is transferred back to his own university and, anyway, two years with him is enough.'

'Sensei, you haven't written about Takeshi at all in this paper.'

'He is in the next chapter. He is sorry when Michiko leaves his house. He is far too busy to spend time on a love affair but after a while he starts meeting hostesses from the mizu shōbai. That is nice for him and doesn't take too much time.'

'What about their weekends at Atami twice a year?'

'They are very good. Michiko enjoys them, even during her love affair with the American professor, because she is interested to experience the difference. Takeshi enjoys them because he is still in love with Michiko.'

'You mean that Michiko is now no longer in love with Takeshi?'

'Of course she is, but her heart is big enough for two loves at the same time.'

'That's magnanimous of her! What happens next?'

### YEARS 10–15    TOGETHER

'Next they are reunited at the end of the separation. Takeshi is now forty and Michiko thirty-five. They live together for five years but I haven't yet written about it. It's not as interesting as when they are apart.'

## YEARS 15-20    SEPARATION

The first extracts on this period described the feelings of Takeshi, now forty-five. Whereas he had been sorry to see Michiko leave his house the first time, on this occasion he was relieved. Michiko, at forty, had become rather difficult to live with, working extremely hard in her medical practice, neglecting household management, not guiding the maids as she should, and even forgetting to order adequate food for his meals.

He was looking forward to restoring order to his household, upgrading the quality of his table and enjoying the variety of pleasures offered by the floating world. He was also looking forward to the absence of a busy, irritable woman who used his house like a hotel.

Michiko, on the other hand, while not wishing to renege on the contract, did not really feel like moving out of the large and comfortable house with its extensive garden (extensive in Tokyo terms, that is, in that a fairly small area had been skilfully transformed into a replica of lakes and mountains by the artistic placing of rocks, pine trees and small waterfalls).

Her aparto in Azabu seemed smaller to her than it had before and in fact the space available for living had been reduced by the necessity to expand the rooms used for her medical practice.

Nevertheless she moved out once again and threw herself into the social whirl, skiing during the winter and travelling abroad with friends. She met another gaijin, this time a handsome White Russian with a dynamic libido. He was the owner of a restaurant which also turned out to contain a sex club for rich Japanese, and she was introduced into this heady atmosphere by the Russian. There were many members from cinema and television and she had a variety of sexual encounters, with both single and multiple partners.

Andrew questioned Nakajima on this.

'Sensei, do such things as sex clubs exist and, if they do, how do you know about them?'

'They certainly do exist, Paton-san. My own husband told me about one that was on the top floor of a restaurant where he was working. He accidentally opened the wrong door one night and saw what was happening with his own eyes.'

'But how is it kept out of the newspapers?'

'Paton-san does not read the Japanese newspapers. Sometimes there are references, or hints, to these things. Especially in the weekly magazines there are stories about the sex clubs, but the journalists are very careful not to embarrass important people.'

'You mean politicians and business tycoons?'

'Yes, and also prominent people whose faces are well known to the public.'

'In your novel, sensei, is there ever any leak to the press?'

'Not a word at first, although the members are almost all from show business, not from politics. Michiko finds it exciting to be with people whose faces appear on the cinema and television screens.'

'Nakajima-sensei, you are a constant source of amazement to me. What would your church friends think if they knew you were writing a book like this?'

Nakajima put her fan over her mouth and laughed. She made no reply but behind her glasses her eyes twinkled merrily.

'Anyway, what did you mean by "not at first"?' asked Andrew.

'I meant that towards the end of the separation a journalist, pretending to be a poet, becomes a member of the sex club and begins writing about it, not openly, but by innuendo, in order to sell his magazine articles.'

'And then?'

'Then one of the members, a film director so famous as to be almost a national treasure, exerts great pressure on the magazine publishing the stories and succeeds in stopping them. But the sex club has to be disbanded.'

## YEARS 20-25   TOGETHER

Takeshi, by now fifty years of age, had still not had any serious liaison. He had enjoyed their bi-annual weekends at Atami and had noticed that Michiko had become more skilled in the art of love. This should have been grounds for enthusiasm at the prospect of her return to his house in Yotsuya but he was, in fact, less than enthusiastic. The hostesses in the mizu shōbai were also highly skilled and they had the advantage of being available on demand.

Takeshi had become more and more set in his ways. His routine was well oiled and, when Michiko finally returned, he found her presence an intrusion. She, for her part, was well pleased to take up her married state once again.

Nakajima's narrative, however, did not resume until the expiration of the period of togetherness.

## YEARS 25-30   SEPARATION

It was some weeks before Nakajima handed Andrew the extracts from the final part of the novel. She had, she said, been undecided on the development of the plot and now confessed to doubts about her original intentions. It appeared that the characters had taken things into their own hands. They had begun to subvert her plot, shaping it to their own fancy, regardless of her wishes.

'It is rather weird, Paton-san,' she confided to Andrew, 'but I don't seem to be able to prevent them from doing it.'

'Doing what, exactly?'

'*Setsumei shinikui, desu ne.*' (It's difficult to explain.) However, she went on to explain it very well. Takeshi was now fifty-five and Michiko fifty. Takeshi had been counting the days until his wife's departure for the third time. Michiko had become very tiresome. She had continual difficulties with her medical practice arising from her habit of going away on holidays and leaving it in the hands of temporary replacements. Every time she did this, something unpleasant happened and she lost some of her patients. She blamed the new generation of doctors. They had no sense of devotion and responsibility, she said. They were too frivolous and interested in just having a good time.

'It sounds to me as if Michiko has been like that herself.'

'Of course, Paton-san, that is true. But she observes it in others, not in herself.'

It also appeared that Michiko had begun to regret not having had children. She was still a very handsome woman but had become harder in the face. She often wore a worried look and concentrated more on money than she used to.

Her first adventure in the new separation period was to take a much younger lover, a man of twenty-five, exactly half her age. The relationship was relatively happy for three reasons. First, Michiko paid for everything, the hotels, the meals, the trips by plane, train or car, and gave him regular pocket-money. Second, she was very experienced sexually and he was not, so she was able to lead him, to their mutual satisfaction. Third, they were both keen skiers.

The young man regarded Michiko almost as an earth mother who provided for him and on whose by now ample body he wallowed joyfully. Far from realising that he was giving her what she wanted, he was astonished that such a well-known doctor should take notice of him. He was very proud of her achievements. It seemed to Andrew, as he worked on the translation, that this young man was an exceptionally nice person. He was well educated, with a university degree, but his own family had disappeared in a manner not explained in the text and he was alone in the world, working as a waiter in a restaurant.

Unfortunately for them both, after the idyll had lasted almost two years, he became infatuated with a hostess in the nightclub on the floor above the restaurant and his ardour for Michiko cooled. At the instigation of the hostess, who was by now his lover, he asked Michiko to buy him a car. She had noticed his change in attitude and accused him of becoming venal. Nevertheless she gave him a small Honda car in which he and the hostess had a serious accident. The young man was killed but the hostess escaped unharmed and inherited the car and all Michiko's other gifts.

Michiko's next adventure, some time after the shock of this accident had subsided, was with her third gaijin. She had decided that gaijin were her best choice, because affairs with them were always of limited duration—they never seemed to remain in Japan indefinitely.

This gaijin was an Englishman, a married man separated from his wife who remained in London. He spoke no Japanese but, fortunately, Michiko's English was quite good. He also was a good skier, and it was on the snowfields that they met. But he drank excessively. At first Michiko drank along with him but she soon found that it affected her work and she reduced her intake. The love affair lasted about a year and then simply petered out.

Michiko continued to meet Takeshi every six months for their weekend at Atami but she noticed during the last couple of years of their separation that he seemed less and less interested in her sexually. She put this down to the fact that by now he was fifty-nine years of age.

'Is she right in this assumption, sensei?' Andrew asked Nakajima. 'I can only guess, because that is as far as this extract goes.'

'Here is another page for you to translate, Paton-san. But in the meantime, there is no need for you to be in suspense, so I shall answer your question. The answer is, no, she is not right. After all, fifty-nine is still a young age for that sort of thing.'

It transpired that the real reason for Takeshi's coolness towards Michiko was that, for the first time since their contract began, he had fallen in love with another woman. Her name was Ayako. She was fifteen years younger than Takeshi, ten years younger than Michiko, and had led a completely different life. She had been married young and her husband had recently died.

What Michiko did not know at that time was that Ayako had moved into Takeshi's house in Yotsuya and was living openly with him. They were very happy.

# THE FIVE-YEAR MARRIAGE CONTRACT

## YEAR 30   THE DEBACLE

The last pages Andrew was given to translate concerned the final year of the third separation. In the last months of the year Takeshi had advised Michiko that he did not want her in his house again and that she should stay in her aparto in Azabu.

'Michiko might even enjoy that. She always seems to want her own freedom,' commented Andrew.

'She wants it when *she* wants it, Paton-san, not when Takeshi wants it. I told you I found the characters had begun to take their fate into their own hands.'

In fact Michiko had been looking forward to the end of the separation. It was not that she had grown too old and too fat to attract other men. On the contrary, she had recently renewed her old affair with the Russian restaurant-owner, the organiser of the erstwhile sex club, had lost most of her surplus weight and had even made one or two visits to a new sex club where she was given proof that she was still attractive to both sexes.

'That's what I mean,' said Andrew. 'She doesn't need to go back to Takeshi.'

'Ah, but she does, Paton-san. She is most anxious to renew her marriage because she wants to retire from her medical practice and be supported by her husband. She has always spent the money she earned and if she continues to live in her extravagant way she will have to work forever. She really wants to revive her marriage and amend the old contract.'

'And Takeshi wants to amend the contract in a different way, of course.'

'No, he wants to stick to the contract and get a divorce, which is provided for in it. He wants to marry Ayako. She has three children of whom he has grown very fond. They have now come to live in his large house in Yotsuya and it often rings with laughter and activity. One of Ayako's children is a dentist who has just got married and the other two, both girls, are at university. Takeshi has found a ready-made and congenial family.'

'So what happens at the end of the novel?'

Nakajima looked pensive.

'I don't know yet,' she said. 'It is the characters who have been manipulating me, not the other way around. But from the way they are behaving at present, the end should not be hard to guess, should it?'

# 17
# THE SHŌGATSU PAY-OFF

On his arrival at the hotel in Sapporo, Andrew changed his booking from a single to a double room and informed the manager that his companion was already in Sapporo and would join him that night. The manager noted this and tactfully refrained from asking the companion's name. It was one of the city's largest and most expensive hotels and, as such, had a policy of not allowing guests to bring girls to their rooms, unless, of course, they were also registered as guests.

It was winter time and Sapporo was white with snow. That evening Andrew was invited out by his company's Hokkaido representative, with two of their largest clients. After dinner in a restaurant of distinction they went to a nightclub.

It was not a nightclub in the Western sense. The décor was more that of a very large loungeroom, quietly furnished, with armless chairs side by side around low tables. There were paintings on the walls, shrubs in pots dotted around, thick carpets, white-coated waiters and dozens of very beautiful hostesses, some in kimono, some in Western dress. At one side of the room there was a four-piece orchestra grouped around a grand piano and a small parquet floor for dancing. The whole effect was of good taste.

Andrew and his Japanese friends were led to a table in a corner and after a few minutes they were assigned five or six hostesses. The conversation flared up immediately, like a brush fire. The girls chattered in Japanese and laughed and giggled. The men teased them and they teased the men—although this teasing was not merely verbal. The sexual horseplay common in even expensive nightclubs was one of the reasons for their existence.

Although this club resembled a loungeroom in a large private home, the gestures and intimacies were exactly those that could not take place at an ordinary social occasion. But then, as Andrew had long since learned, the whole function of the floating world was to provide a release, an escape, from the web of everyday obligations and good behaviour.

The hostess on Andrew's right, a young girl of perhaps twenty, dressed in a Japanese kimono, turned to the other members of the party and a mischievous twinkle lit up her whole face. She announced that she was curious to know whether gaijin were the same size as Japanese.

Everyone else seemed to think that this was a subject worthy of research and Andrew found a hand in his lap. With the large right sleeve of her kimono she covered her left hand while it purposefully prepared Andrew for the test. The resulting verdict brought roars of delighted laughter and one of the waiters arrived carrying a new tray of drinks.

Andrew invited her to dance. Her body under the kimono was soft and she pressed close to him, with the result that the test could just as well have been made on the dance floor.

Her name was Atsuko. They danced several times and she made it clear to him with her eyes and her smile of complicity that his recurring embarrassment was not unwelcome to her. He asked her to come to his hotel after the club closed. She agreed. But, she said, he must not wait for her here. He must leave with the others and go, as is usual in Japan, to another club, cabaret or bar and she would meet him at twelve midnight, alone, at the Kikuyama Supper Club. The Kikuyama, she assured him, was well known to any Sapporo taxi-driver. She particularly did not want any of the other girls in this place to know she was meeting him.

Atsuko left Andrew's party shortly afterwards to go to another table. Hostesses were often rotated in this manner, disappearing suddenly, without notice, sometimes returning later, sometimes not. Atsuko only reappeared briefly to join the other hostesses in bowing them a friendly but impersonal sayonara.

The next place was noisier, more animated and somewhat

vulgar but amusing. When they left it at half past eleven, Andrew made an excuse about wanting to walk by himself, bid them all goodnight and escaped from the taxi they had ordered.

He found the Kikuyama Supper Club without difficulty and sat at a table close to the door where he could see everyone coming in. Atsuko was late. The Kikuyama band was loudly and exuberantly beating out music.

The tiny dance floor was half full. Two girls were dancing together. An enormous Japanese in a fancy white suit was taking his partner back to a table where another girl was waiting. There were lovers and one middle-aged couple seemingly mesmerised by each other. There was a girl dancing without her shoes and a lanky American with a little Japanese girl coming up to his diaphragm.

Beyond the dance floor the tables were in discreet obscurity. A sign at the door had said that the Kikuyama Supper Club was open from 9 p.m. to 4 a.m.

When Atsuko appeared at the door, searching short-sightedly in the gloom, she was wearing a large fur coat over her kimono. The effect of the heavy folds of the obi at her back was to push this overcoat up and out, as though she were wearing a school satchel on her back. Andrew thought the result was unfortunate.

There was no hint that something was worrying her while she ate, no mention of it in the taxi and nothing led Andrew to suspect it, until they had reached his room in the hotel and had hung up the offending fur coat which so deformed her appearance. Then, as he was about to kiss her, she squirmed out of his grasp and said she must soon leave, since she had important business at 2 a.m. Andrew was not sure whether this was meant as a polite brush-off or was genuine. He did not understand it at all and therefore took the direct route, followed his instincts, and kissed her. She kissed superbly, a fact he noted all the more carefully because it was often written that Japanese women did not kiss. But what, he wondered, do the people who write travel books really know about such things, other than what Japanese image makers tell them?

The kiss seemed to decide Atsuko as well, because she did not resist his attempts to undo her obi and helped him disengage the strings and ribbons holding the kimono. He soon discovered that he would never have been able to undress her without her help. The cords and knots were endless, the layers multitudinous. In his present state the situation was exasperating.

The last layer was a kind of half slip, like a sarong. He opened it. She wore neither panties nor bra. Her body was lovely, much smaller than it had seemed to be in the kimono. He lifted her and half fell with her onto the bed, in a protracted kiss, her arms tightly around him.

They created a dream around their love-making. It was as if it were the hundredth time, not the first. She would kiss him joyfully, almost elatedly, and then her lips would seem to lose the power to kiss and she would take his head on her shoulder, her fingers holding the back of his neck, and utter a long, broken cry. Many times this happened until, after they had been lying quietly together, not moving, something, a noise outside perhaps, broke the spell and Atsuko looked at the travelling clock on the bedside table.

'I must go now,' she said.

'But no,' Andrew protested. 'Call your friends, or whoever it is, and say you can't come.'

'No, Andrew-chan, you do not understand. I must go to my aparto and wait for a phone call at two o'clock. There is nobody else there to take the call. It is very important. You can come and stay in my aparto if you like and we will wait together.'

The argument went on for some minutes but Atsuko was adamant. She re-applied all the layers and cords and sashes of her kimono and obi and finally she was dressed. But she would not tell Andrew the reason for the phone call at 2 a.m.

There had been no question of money and Andrew was wondering how to give her a present delicately when she suddenly apologised for leaving so soon, promised to meet him the following night at midnight at the Kikuyama Supper Club, kissed him lovingly, and swept out the door, leaving Andrew standing naked and slightly confused.

## THE SHŌGATSU PAY-OFF

The next day was like the first day of a new love. Andrew felt infused with an unreasoning gaiety. He could not concentrate on his assignment. He walked in the snow and was happy to feel it fluttering coldly against his face. The sun had come out and the mountains around the town glistened whitely. In the Odori-koen, the park which runs through the heart of Sapporo city, there was a display of snow sculpture, giant models in snow of castles, heroes and demons.

He lived through the day in expectation of the night and at midnight he was there at the Kikuyama Supper Club, at the same table, watching the door.

Atsuko came in almost immediately, her kimono once again hidden by the thick fur coat. She was frowning.

'Quick,' she said, 'we must go. There are some other girls from the club coming.'

'Don't you want anything to eat?'

'No, I'll eat later. Let's go.'

The head waiter accepted the situation with good grace. There was no bill.

In the taxi Atsuko did not hold Andrew's hand.

They were once again in his room and he was about to kiss her, when she broke away.

'Andrew-chan, later, please. I must go out again soon. But I'll come back, I promise.'

'But why go out? We've just arrived.'

'Yes, I know. First I make a phone call. I must call this girl. She owes me money and tonight she will pay.'

'Good God, Atsuko. Call her and tell her you'll meet her at nine o'clock in the morning. Now is not the time to collect money.'

'Yes, it is. Tonight she gets paid by her club. By nine in the morning somebody else will catch her money. Let me explain.'

It transpired that Atsuko had lent money everywhere. This was the twenty-eighth of December. Following an old tradition, all debts should be paid before the Shōgatsu holidays, beginning on the first of January. During these last three frantic days Atsuko had to get out and 'catch' her money, as she put it.

She sat at the dressing table beside the bed with the telephone in one hand and a pencil in the other, calling some numbers written in her notebook. Her elegant kimono, her piled up coiffure, her red and gold obi and the young, beautiful face all seemed to Andrew totally incongruous with the determined money-lender inside, bent on tracking down her debtors in the early morning hours. He imagined her returning with her purse bulging with notes.

He sat beside her while she worked.

'Atsuko,' he said very softly, so as not to disturb the financier deep in thought.

'*Hai.*'

'Atsuko, how much interest do you charge when you lend?'

'What is "interest"?'

'You know, when you borrow a hundred at the bank, you must pay back 107 or 108 at the end of the year. How much do you charge?'

'Me? Nothing, of course.'

'Nothing?'

'Nothing.'

'Then why do you lend your money?'

'Andrew-chan, you do not understand. The *yoru no hito* [the night people], like hostesses, musicians, you know, all the people in the mizu shōbai, almost never have money. When they get it, they lend it or spend it or pay someone back.'

'But why do you lend without interest?'

'Because sometimes I need to borrow, too. If I don't lend sometimes, I can't borrow. Also because I know how it feels to need money quickly.'

'This girl you're phoning now, why did she borrow?'

'She was sick and couldn't work.'

'How much did she borrow from you?'

'40 000 yen.'

Atsuko was speaking absently, with her back to Andrew, as she dialled the telephone operator. The number she wanted had been engaged every time. Now she was connected. A quick conversation followed, fixing the time and the place. Then she rose, picked up the heavy fur coat and began putting it on.

Andrew thought of protesting but what was the use? He felt as if all this had no connection with him, as if it were another world quite independent of him.

'I will come back at two o'clock,' Atsuko said.

'And will you stay then, or will you be off again at two-thirty?'

'No, truly, I will stay. All night. We will have breakfast together.'

She smiled and Andrew noted that it was the first time she had smiled that evening. Where was the dream of a new love? This was his last night in Sapporo. Tomorrow he would go to Shikotsuko and later to Akano, one of the coldest but most beautiful parts of Hokkaido.

He tried to hold her in his arms but she wriggled out. He sensed that this was no time to make a pretence of forcing her to kiss him and let her go.

'I will come back at two o'clock,' she said again and opened the door, preoccupied and unsmiling.

'Yes, of course.' Andrew closed the door behind her. He would wait, but she would not come. He knew she would not come.

Nevertheless, he waited. He waited until 4 a.m., imagining her going from bar to supper club, from café to café, searching for the girl who had already given the 40 000 yen to her lover, or her landlady, or had hidden it in a box to spend on clothes the next day.

He waited and thought of this futile search and of the money that he, Andrew, had intended to give her, discreetly, generously, if she had ever stopped still long enough, if she had ever stopped thinking of her own money long enough for a present to have been given.

He lay in bed and waited and thought. He thought of himself and his wish to spend money on love, of Atsuko who wanted money but had no time for love.

He thought of the snow on his face that morning and his

delight in his discovery of Atsuko and the sharp pain at his loss of her and of the fleeting passage of life and the impermanence of the floating world.

His mind raced on until his thoughts became confused and stupid and he slipped into a fretful sleep.

# 18
# EPILOGUE—HIGH BLOOD

Andrew was on leave in Sydney when the news came of Nakajima's death. She had always spoken of her 'high blood', one of the phrases from her very limited English vocabulary meaning high blood pressure. In addition to that, her heart had been in poor condition for years. Something must have suddenly happened in her plump little body to set off an internal accident that led to the stroke from which she never regained consciousness. It had been apparently painless, for her, if not for those close to her.

Six years before he had been dragged unwillingly to Japan. Now he returned sadly to a country grown dear to him. During those six years Nakajima had opened up for him her personal vision of her country and its people. Like all personal visions it was far less than all-encompassing but it had shown him the way to wider vistas that he himself had to explore.

He was met at the airport by Nakajima's nephew, Yoshio, who drove Andrew to his apartment. Andrew remembered when Yoshio had acquired the car. Three years previously Nakajima had saved up enough money to take an overseas holiday, a thing she had dreamt about for years. But Yoshio had been involved in an accident in his automobile, which had not been adequately insured, and Nakajima had given him her holiday money to buy a new one. With cheerful composure she had gone back to dreaming of her trip. Perhaps next time, she had said, perhaps next time I will go away.

Yoshio told Andrew that Nakajima's husband had taken the loss very badly and was in the country with a distant relative.

They passed Hibiya Park with the large nondescript building at one end of it where Andrew had gone on several occasions to hear Nakajima play the koto in Sunday afternoon concerts.

At the first concert he had found it difficult to distinguish her among the rows of women koto players. Then he had spotted her and waved. As he drove on with Yoshio towards his home in Roppongi, he saw her again in his mind, looking down at the koto and pretending that the eager gaijin in the audience was waving unbecomingly at someone else. She had scolded him afterwards. The koto, she had said, is played with decorum. Waving is a sign of excessive exuberance on such an august occasion. A small movement of the fingers, which she demonstrated, would have been adequate.

He looked around him through the car windows at all the signs in kanji characters now quite familiar to him, like old friends whose acquaintance one has struggled to make, and remembered Nakajima trying to teach him calligraphy. But he had not been gifted at it. He could write with a pen, he could paint with a brush, but he could not put the two together and achieve the flow and rhythm and the darkening and lightening effects which the brush made when Nakajima held it.

A few evenings after his return to Tokyo, Andrew found Obata-sensei in the Munich beer-hall and told him about Nakajima's death. Obata was sympathetic. He was his usual urbane self. He had been studying Zen, he told Andrew, drinking his beer.

'Is beer compatible with Zen?' Andrew asked.

'In my case everything is. I'm studying it but not practising it; I am too far from being an ascetic. But the ideas of Zen help and meditation does, too. I have practised a bit of that. That might have helped your Nakajima-sensei with her "high blood".'

'It is strange the sense of loss I feel,' Andrew said.

'Not strange at all, Paton-san. Love takes many forms. Have you ever asked yourself which is the greater loss: the disappearance from your life of someone you love or someone who loves you?'

'Not specifically.'

'The difference is that, speaking as a cynical old man of the world and referring to spouses and friends, not children, you may be able sooner or later to replace the person you loved, but your world is forever diminished by the loss of the person who loved you. In that case the replacement is beyond your power.'

How strange, Andrew thought, and yet how true, that his world should be forever diminished by the loss of a little old lady with brightly hennaed hair who had shuffled across his office to meet him six years earlier. He suddenly remembered exactly how she had looked and how he had misjudged her.

Upstairs at street level the crowds swirling around Ginza Yon-chome were still the same. The neon lights were flashing and beckoning, the pachinko parlours were clattering and the street vendors were shouting their wares. Andrew walked slowly through all this movement, thinking of Obata's words, without noticing where he was going.